Why in the world had she let him kiss her?

Oh, she'd wanted it. Had ached for the touch of his hands, for that exclusive look from his ginger-snap eyes, the look that told a woman she was special. Desirable. That she had his sole attention.

And what a kiss it had been, far beyond any and all of her expectations.

But it was wrong, wrong to yearn, to allow the intimacy that would shift their relationship, that would make living under the same roof with any sort of easiness next to impossible.

She'd made a vow to marry another man. Why was it so hard to remember that? Her mind immediately supplied the answer.

It was because of a sexy guy with killer dimples, a man who could exasperate her...*thrill* her.

Dear Reader,

In a tiny western town of Grazer's Corners, something is happening.... All over the town square, weddings are in the air—and the town's most eligible bachelors are running for cover!

Three popular American Romance authors have put together a rollicking good time in The Brides of Grazer's Corners. On the satin-pump heels of Jacqueline Diamond's THE COWBOY & THE SHOTGUN BRIDE comes Mindy Neff's A BACHELOR FOR THE BRIDE—and next month Charlotte Maclay brings you THE HOG-TIED GROOM.

You're invited to all three weddings.... Who'll catch the bouquet next?

Happy reading!

Debra Matteucci
Senior Editor & Editorial Coordinator
Harlequin
300 E. 42nd St.
New York, NY 10017

A Bachelor
for the Bride

MINDY NEFF

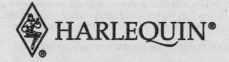

HARLEQUIN®

TORONTO • NEW YORK • LONDON
AMSTERDAM • PARIS • SYDNEY • HAMBURG
STOCKHOLM • ATHENS • TOKYO • MILAN • MADRID
PRAGUE • WARSAW • BUDAPEST • AUCKLAND

For three very special friends:
Charlotte Lobb, Joan Sweeney and Susan Liepitz.
Thanks for your friendship and support, for the hugs,
hand-holding and swearwords and, most important of all,
for *never* doubting. You're the best, guys! And to
Jackie Hyman, the instigator of the Kidnapped Brides.

ISBN 0-373-16739-3

A BACHELOR FOR THE BRIDE

Chapter One

It was a dangerous thing to be at loose ends on the eve of your wedding, Jordan thought. It left a girl wide-open to second thoughts, for restlessness to creep in.

Debating her impulsive decision, she sat behind the wheel of her sporty Mazda convertible, hesitating over turning the key.

Friday night.

In twenty-four hours she'd be Mrs. Randall Latrobe.

Discontent nudged her, sending her insides tumbling. Since Pastor Lewis had had a prior commitment, they'd veered from the traditional and held the wedding rehearsal and dinner last night...which had suited Randall just fine. It left him free this evening to wine and dine some Republican bigwig from Modesto.

She wondered if he'd have been so quick to leave her to her own devices if he'd known what she had in mind.

She stared at the sprawling ranch-style house in front of her with its white stucco and wood accents. So familiar, she thought. So comfortable. Yet, after tonight, nothing would be quite the same. She wouldn't be returning to her childhood home as a single woman.

Dear Lord, was she making the right decision?

Feeling unsettled by the idea of change, she absorbed the sight of her surroundings like a thirsty sapling in anticipation of drought. Beyond the house, dipping into the valley, were the vineyards. Ever since the fire some fifteen years back, the vines to the south had been stingy with their fruit. To the east, though, behind the stables, the crops flourished.

Still, it was a case of too little too late. By the time money was realized from that yield, the estate could very well be in foreclosure.

Jordan was determined not to let that happen.

By marrying Randall, she'd make sure Daddy would get the loan he so desperately needed to keep them afloat—a loan that would safeguard her beloved stables.

For that alone, Jordan would sacrifice almost anything.

And marriage wasn't such a bad deal, she told herself. It was time she settled down, anyway. At twenty-seven, she was by no means "on the shelf," as Agatha Flintstone was fond of saying—a term gleaned from her coveted romance novels—but neither was she getting younger. Jordan wanted children, a home.

Randall was a good choice—"husband material," according to just about everybody in town. They'd been dating for more than a year and he'd proved steady, loyal and relatively attentive. So what if their relationship lacked passion. There was an easiness to it that would suit her just fine.

Besides, Randall's busy schedule and involvement in the community would give her the space she needed, leave her plenty of free time to pursue her dream of becoming a top horse-breeder.

Although he didn't share her enthusiasm for her horses, he wouldn't stand in her way. It was no secret that he had his eye on the political arena, and Jordan, with her spotless reputation, would make him a good wife.

Give and take, she thought. They'd both benefit from the union.

The call of a peacock pierced the stillness of the night, making her jump, its eerie cry sounding like a woman screaming "Help!"

Help!

The plea echoed through her mind, pounding through her system.

Her restlessness grew.

Just once, she thought. One night to be somebody she wasn't. What could it hurt?

Like a storm raging inside her, the thought kept flashing across her brain, taunting her, beckoning....

Because, inside her "I-aim-to-please" exterior lurked a wild child. Well hidden, to be sure; rarely let out to play, but there nonetheless.

Making up her mind, she twisted the key in the ignition.

At the sound of the engine, the porch light blinked. An instant later, Lydia Grazer stepped out the front door.

"Jordan?" she called, her voice sounding puzzled. "Did you square things away with the photographer?"

Damn. She didn't want to think about any more

wedding stuff tonight. She wanted one night of free-dom—freedom from decision making, from the stress and tedious details that went along with a pseudo-high-society wedding.

So far she'd done everything by the book, right down to the prerequisite bachelorette party—a calm, correct little get-together at Sandra's house. Not a beefcake male stripper in sight. That would be be-neath the country-club set.

Her hands tightened around the steering wheel. Was one blessed night of autonomy too much to ask for?

But obligation and responsibility were ingrained in her. It wasn't the photographer's fault she was feeling restless and rebellious. And she liked Charity Arden, knew she was struggling to make a go of her photography business while freelancing for the *Grazer Gazette,* as well as working her family's pig farm and raising a seven-year-old son by herself.

Added to that, since Kate Bingham had been nabbed right from the altar at her wedding in an odd shoot-em-up fiasco just last week, Charity's finances were probably suffering. A botched wedding meant no photos and no money for the talented-yet-struggling photographer.

"Jordan?" Lydia called again, taking a step down from the porch.

Adrenaline surged and Jordan automatically scooted lower in the bucket seat, feeling like a schoolgirl caught sneaking out of the dorm past cur-few. Although her black cashmere sweater covered her upper body, it wouldn't do for her mother to get a glimpse of the rest of her outfit.

What little there was of it.

"It's taken care of, Mother." Or would be with a phone call.

"Where are you going?"

She hated to lie, but she needed this one night more than anything—like a last meal before an execution.

And if she didn't stop thinking about her wedding to Randall Latrobe that way, she'd be in big trouble.

"I'm meeting Charity in town. I'll be in early." Twenty-seven and still accounting for her whereabouts, she thought. As for the fib…well, maybe it wouldn't be a fib after all.

Putting the car in gear before her mother could delay her further, Jordan headed out of the circular drive that wound past pristine fences and paddocks where horses grazed. Her prized stallion, Honor Bleu, was bedded down in the stables for the night.

Bleu was the only point she'd been adamant about while everyone else was orchestrating her life and her marriage.

Where she went, Bleu went. No discussion.

Randall wasn't crazy about her dedication to her horses—neither was her father, for that matter—but she'd refused to budge. And, until Randall could have stables built at their new home, Jordan would be spending plenty of time at her parents' estate.

Provided they didn't lose it to the bank.

But she wasn't going to think about that tonight.

Once on the two-lane blacktop, she picked up her cellular phone and dialed Charity Arden's number.

"Charity? It's Jordan Grazer. I know you wanted to go over the photo layout for tomorrow, but I've got a schedule conflict. Could you meet me at Gatlin's just outside of town?" They'd already postponed the meeting once due to the date change of the rehearsal.

"Gatlin's?" Charity was clearly astonished. The club catered to a different clientele—definitely not a spot a local debutante would patronize.

"Yes. Do you know how to get there?"

"Sure. My brother's home, so he can watch Donnie for me. I should be able to make it in about a half hour."

"Great. We'll hash out the wedding-photo details over drinks. Thanks, Charity."

She ended the call and barreled down the road, her tires hitting a patch of gravel and kicking up clouds of dust that swirled murkily in the beams of her headlights. Warm June air whipped her hair in the open convertible as stars sparkled like a canopy of diamonds overhead. The sweet smell of alfalfa mixed with the more pungent scent of cattle ranches perfumed the air.

Feeling freer by the mile, she steadied the wheel with her knees and peeled off her conservative sweater, reveling in the way the breeze caressed her skin above her low-necked top.

She really did love this locality. Living on the outskirts of Grazer's Corners was like being in the country. There were wide-open spaces and plenty of unincorporated areas to ride horses. There were changes, yes, and growth, but big-city developers had yet to discover their sleepy, central-California paradise. And even if they did, her father, Maynard Grazer—who liked to think he owned the whole town because it was named after his forefathers—would pitch a fit. He wouldn't stand still for tract houses in correct earth tones gobbling up their farm-lands, overpopulating their slice of utopia.

Once past the Fun House Candy factory, Jordan rounded the final curve leading into the heart of Grazer's Corners. In order to get to Gatlin's, she had to pass through town. Nerves crowded in her throat and she pressed the accelerator, hoping to zip through without detection.

The problem with small towns was that every-body knew everybody else. Although the business owners practically rolled up the sidewalks at five o'clock, the Good Eats Diner would still be open.

And if they saw her convertible pass, people would speculate as to why Jordan Grazer was dressed as she was—and without her fiancé at her side—on the eve of her wedding.

Thankfully, she breezed right through the only stoplight in town—the one Moose Harmon had lob-bied to install, right in front of his department store.

She nearly ducked as she passed the Good Eats and spared a thought for her excessive speed. Then again, there was little worry she'd get a ticket. Sher-iff Brockner had moved up his retirement date and left town in somewhat of a huff, claiming he'd much rather fuss with his gardening and hothouse orchids than put up with any more local politics. And the temporary sheriff-elect, Kate Bingham, was still missing.

Lordy, bandits and kidnappings in Grazer's Cor-ners! Maybe they were closer to big-city change than Jordan realized.

Pulling into the crowded parking lot of Gatlin's, she parked her Mazda next to a shiny Harley, sud-denly assailed with second thoughts. A far cry from the elegant country club, Gatlin's catered to a different crowd.

The place was a meat market for singles. She'd been here once on a dare—"uptown girls slumming," Sandra and Jewel had said.

This time was for herself, though.

Squaring her shoulders, she got out of the car. Tonight there would be no images to uphold, no acts to put on.

Just a wild, let-your-hair-down sort of night.

One night before she became the oh-so-respectable Mrs. Randall Latrobe.

The band was loud, the crowd festive and humming with anticipation. She shook her jet-black hair over her shoulders, smoothed her animal-print mini-skirt, and gave a tug to the shimmering top that scooped low over her breasts. Four-inch heels hoisted her up to an impressive, sexy six feet.

She felt the appreciative stares as she made her way through the crowd. Insides quaking, yet thrilled with herself, her nerve, her uncharacteristic gumption in seizing the moment, she ordered a beer, leaned against the counter and sipped straight from the bottle, her lipstick leaving a ring of crimson around the mouth of the dark glass.

"Hey there, good-lookin'. Where've you been all my life?"

She glanced toward the sound of the voice. It was an awful, trite line. She started to shut him down with a practiced look, then thought better of it. Dressed like an urban cowboy, the guy looked decent enough. Besides, she wasn't out to go home with anybody. Just to have a good time. She wanted

to dance the night away—with anyone who would
ask.

And if they didn't ask, she'd do the asking herself
or dance alone.

She grinned, sauntered forward and said, "I've
been here, darlin'...looking for you."

The guy's Adam's apple bobbed and his shoulders went back. Obviously he thought he'd just gotten lucky. The deejay cranked up one of Rod Stewart's hits from the eighties as though he'd read her
mood.

Yes, like the words of the song, she was feeling
sexy.

"Want to dance, cowboy?" Without checking to
see if he followed, she moved onto the dance floor
and picked up the rhythm. This was one of those
nights when she knew that confidence and sex appeal radiated from her. She felt it, projected it, reveled in it.

Her height in the heels alone drew attention, as
did the expanse of toned thighs and calves revealed
by the miniskirt. She was the center of attention.

Male attention.

The image was so far removed from who she really was. And Jordan loved it. Loved this dangerous,
crazy, walk on the wild side.

It was while she was laughing, head thrown back,
that she spotted him.

Sitting at a table. Alone. His eyes tracking her
every sway and shimmy.

Recognition slammed into her and she nearly lost
her balance on her four-inch heels.

Or *was* it recognition? She hadn't seen Tanner

Caldwell in ten years. And it wasn't likely that he would ever return to Grazer's Corners.

Not after the way her family had treated him.

Still, something in this brooding bad-boy's look called to her, held her spellbound...made her yearn.

Her steps, fluid and graceful before, lost the rhythm of the beat. Rod Stewart still wailed on about being sexy and letting somebody know. Adrenaline shot what little alcohol she'd consumed straight to her brain, making her bold—even though her insides trembled like mad.

It was as though the room had receded, as though they were the only two in the dim, smoky club. Her gaze locked on to his, deliberately, challenging him to get up and come across the room.

Was he feeling this same mesmerizing attraction that she was? "Well, come on, hotshot," she muttered. "Give me a hint."

Let me know if it's really you, or if my eyes are playing tricks.

But he didn't smile. Didn't acknowledge her or give any hint of recognition, just fixed her with a direct, unreadable stare.

And that raised her ire.

She tipped up her beer bottle and took several swigs, her gaze still on the long-haired stranger whose penetrating gaze and shadowed countenance rang such familiar bells.

She rotated her hips in a sultry move meant to entice.

It enticed every man in the room—except one.

Okay, she thought. *I'll play the game.* She wasn't herself tonight, could be anybody she wanted.

Act any way she wanted.

Tomorrow was soon enough to revert to the *real* Jordan Grazer. The "I-aim-to-please," good-girl Jordan Grazer.

A little drunk now, she became bolder. She thanked her cowboy partner sweetly, then left the dance floor, heading for the Tanner look-alike's table.

He never altered his slouchy position. His gaze never wavered. She almost lost her nerve, had an idea this man was more than she could ever handle.

But an incendiary spark of something—something she couldn't put a name to—drove her on.

She couldn't read his expression. It could have been a mask of stone. His eyes neither welcomed nor indicated one way or the other whether he cared that she'd obviously singled him out and was on her way to join him.

He wore boots that were well broken in, tattered Levi's that hugged his lean lower body like a lover, and a black T-shirt that stretched across his broad, muscular shoulders. His dark hair hung long to his shoulders, in the style worn by both rock stars and Hell's Angels.

This guy was definitely rough around the edges— arrogant, yet thrilling to look at. He had a "don't-touch-me" aura that would draw women like a magnet.

An effect Jordan was obviously not immune to.

"Jordan?"

The sound of her name broke the sensual spell like a pinprick in an overinflated balloon. A little disoriented, she dragged her gaze away from the sinfully sexy temptation.

Charity Arden stood a few feet away. Damn.

She'd forgotten all about the scheduled meeting. Jordan didn't want to think about wedding plans. But her innate sense of responsibility penetrated her fog, banishing the allure of bad boys and of acting in a manner that would probably shock the whole town if word got out.

And Charity Arden was part of that town. But Charity wouldn't judge, Jordan realized. She had her own code of ethics that was a far cry from the uppity country-club set's—and she had a seven-year-old son whose father's name she'd adamantly refused to divulge.

And for that strength of character, Jordan admired her. Charity wasn't a woman who'd marry a man if she was having second thoughts.

Like Jordan was.

Thankfully her brain wasn't too pickled from the alcohol to outline a list of photos the Latrobes and Grazers would need.

Half of her giddiness came from the adrenaline rush of seeing Tanner Caldwell.

If it was even him.

"Hi, Charity," Jordan said, changing direction, resisting the urge to glance back over her shoulder— to see if *he* was watching. "You made it. Let's grab a table."

"There's one," the photographer said.

Right next to the walking fantasy in tattered jeans and too-long hair. For some reason, Jordan didn't want to be close enough for him to overhear her talk of wedding plans.

She wanted to be free, available to start something she had no business starting. To see where it would lead.

Taking herself—and her runaway imagination—in hand, she steered Charity to another table and ordered drinks from a passing waitress.

From the corner of her eye, she saw him rise. Her heart slammed against her chest. Would he come to her?

He didn't. Tall and strong, with a loose, easy stride, he disappeared into the crowd.

Now she'd never know for sure if the guy was really Tanner, and that left her feeling unsettled, made her want to drive by the old trailer park where he'd lived, search the streets for him.

A really dumb idea, especially since she was to be married in less than twenty-four hours.

Maybe it was just wishful thinking; maybe she just *wanted* this guy to be him. At seventeen, she'd spun plenty of fantasies around Tanner—dreamed he was her motorcycle Romeo. And she was his Juliet. But because of the strict social barriers between them, that was all she'd been able to do.

Dream from a distance.

Because to get any closer would have put her impeccable reputation at risk.

A reputation she was taking a dire chance with tonight.

Her big plans for the evening suddenly lost their appeal. Although still restless, she now felt empty. She began to regret the impulsiveness of the night out, of the attention-getting miniskirt and bold crimson lipstick.

"Jordan?" Charity touched Jordan's hand. "Everything okay?"

"Yeah. Just wedding jitters. I'm obviously not myself."

Charity grinned. "Hey, every girl's entitled to one wild night…a secret or two."

She realized that the pretty photographer was speaking from personal experience. Charity had a secret—it revolved round a very real, seven-year-old little boy—and suddenly Jordan felt a kinship with the woman.

"How's Donnie?"

"Ornery as ever," Charity said lovingly. "With way too much energy."

"You should bring him out to the ranch sometime and let him ride." Not only did Jordan have prize breeding stock, she also stabled several docile mares for pleasure riding. And one of the charities close to her heart was the school of handicapped children who came out once a month to ride and enjoy the horses.

Thinking about the sweet, innocent faces of those youngsters reminded Jordan of what was important.

Her marriage to Randall.

And the bank loan that would ensure the stables stayed afloat financially…for herself, for the horses she'd rescued that nobody else wanted, and for the children.

Guilt washed over her in scalding waves. She had no business coming to this club, acting wild, spinning fantasies. She knew very well what was expected of her and what she needed to do.

"Maybe I'll take you up on that sometime," Charity said.

Jordan nodded. "Okay, let's run down a list of family members and shots you'll need tomorrow." Even though she felt more than a little light-headed, she poured her beer into a glass and made an effort to sip it like a well-bred lady—though if anyone cared to look closely, they'd see that her dainty sips were more like desperate gulps.

She had an idea she'd have a heck of a hangover during her wedding ceremony.

And fantasies about the *wrong* man on her wedding night.

TANNER KNEW DAMNED WELL he was torturing himself. But when he'd seen the wedding announcement in the paper, he hadn't been able to stay away. The nuptials promised to be some shindig—hell, they'd run the piece in every big-city paper from Los Angeles to San Francisco.

Debutante to Marry Banker.

She didn't look like any bride *he'd* ever seen on the eve of her wedding. And the last place he'd expected to run into her was at Gatlin's. By God, she'd been seducing him with her eyes—in a bar overflowing with people.

People who would no doubt talk.

Although Tanner was immune to gossip, Jordan wasn't. At least, she hadn't been ten years ago.

For the thousandth time, Tanner wondered what he was even doing here. The answer was swift and the same—tormenting himself, yearning for something, *someone,* he couldn't have.

Even knowing she was out of his league, he'd still kept tabs on her over the years, had never been able to completely get her out of his mind.

In her family's eyes, he hadn't been good enough for Jordan Grazer; didn't have the right surname, the right title…didn't have enough money to be accepted into their social circle.

And that was the kicker. Now, at a point in his life when he could rightfully meet the debutante on an equal footing, she was once again out of his reach.

Engaged to marry another man.

Tomorrow.

But he'd had to come, to get one last look. To see if she still affected him so powerfully.

The answer was yes. More than ever.

And it was too late.

Get a grip, man. Swinging his leg over the seat of the Harley, he booted the kickstand, suddenly anxious to get out of town. He should never have come in the first place.

His finger hovered over the Harley's start button. A couple of yokels stood a few feet away, their furtive mannerisms causing him to go on alert. Being a security expert made him suspicious of just about everybody.

And these two were up to something.

They moved closer, practically standing right next to his bike, dismissing him as though he were invisible.

"The broad's worth big bucks. I tell you, it'll be a piece of cake," the short one said. Balding, he'd combed what few strands of hair he actually possessed from a side part that started just above the tip of one big ear.

"So why don't we just take care of it tonight?" This from the middle-aged hippie whose red suspenders drew undue attention to a watermelon-size beer gut.

"Don't be an idiot. The boss wants the *right* audience to notice. We're not exactly in the country-club parking lot, you know."

"I thought we were going to the church."

The little guy rolled his eyes. "Must I lead you by the hand? Here, take this." He passed a slip of paper, grabbed the hippie by the arm and steered him toward an early-sixties minibus.

From then on, Tanner couldn't hear enough to be absolutely certain what was going down, but he thought he heard the word "nab."

Ah, hell. The only rich broad whose name was connected with church and country club was Jordan Grazer.

It appeared his masochism was not going to end just yet. On the off chance that Jordan was in danger, he'd have to set aside his pride and hang around a little while longer—at least until he could report his suspicions to the sheriff. Of course, if Brockner was still running the show, that wouldn't be much help.

The man was as inept as they came.

And the sheriff wouldn't likely place much credence on the word of Tanner Caldwell.

Because in this town, Tanner's name was painted with the same tar-coated brush as that of his drunkard father—the man who'd set a torch to the Grazers' vineyards.

Chapter Two

Feeling a little like a guest at her own wedding—an *invisible* guest—Jordan stared at her attendants. Cory, Jewel and Sandra were hogging the mirror in the tiny room near the back of the Sunday-school wing of the church.

With a hand full of hairpins, Jordan was forced to wade through a pile of discarded clothes and shoes just to get her purse. But she soon found that the little compact she kept there wasn't going to do the trick. She needed both hands free.

"Can one of you help me with my veil?" Three sets of eyes barely flickered in the mirror's reflection.

"Just a sec," Sandra said. "This lipstick's all wrong and it's stained my lips. Where is that remover?" She rummaged through the makeup cases on the small dressing table—the seat reserved for the *bride* to do last-minute touch-ups.

If she'd been the type, Jordan might have sat down and bawled. She felt alone, out of sorts, scared over the decision she'd made that would change her whole life.

And hot. The air conditioner obviously wasn't

working. Already, she could feel the satin of her dress clinging to her skin.

Everything felt wrong, right down to this cramped cubicle they'd been shoved into at the last minute. Pastor Lewis had held his meeting the night before in the Green Room, where the bridal party normally convened, and had claimed it simply wasn't up to standard this morning.

Jordan blew out a weary sigh. Did the old preacher consider *this* one up to standard? There were newspapers on the windows, for pete's sake. Frowning, she did a double take. For a second, she could have sworn she saw the weathered face of a man peering in where the newspapers didn't quite meet over the dusty panes.

Ridiculous.

She was simply overwrought. Wedding jitters.

Added to that, the music blaring out of Sandra's boom box was sending shards of pain through her temples.

This wasn't the way she'd imagined the day would be.

And what was keeping her parents? Since they were so eager for this marriage to take place, it seemed they could at least have had the decency to be early, to wait with her, ease any nerves.

Neither one was in sight. Daddy claimed he had details to see to. Mother was orchestrating the guests.

Needing air, needing a *friend,* Jordan grabbed her veil, her purse and her bouquet of roses, carnations and gardenias and left the room. Charity Arden ought to be around somewhere. Jordan knew that at least *she* would stop long enough to fasten a veil.

With her satin train looped over her arm so she wouldn't trip herself, she peeked into the hallway, then headed in the direction of the main sanctuary, making an effort to stay out of sight. Through the vestibule, she could see that the side doors were open, as were the front. The small church was already bursting with people—predominantly the country-club set. Randall had insisted on a big, splashy affair.

Jordan knew it was costing Daddy money he couldn't afford, but Maynard, too, insisted on keeping up appearances.

Heaven forbid if the good folks of Grazer's Corners should find out he was teetering on the brink of financial disaster.

She caught sight of the photographer and was trying to figure out a way to get the woman's attention when there was a commotion at the side door. Probably one of the guests who'd wandered into the wrong hall. It was hard to tell the front from the side entrance because of the way the church sat on the corner.

"Wrong door," she said.

A short, balding man who looked a little like a penguin in a tux, nudged an aging hippie who wore suspenders rather than the traditional cummerbund under a jacket that had no hope of buttoning over the size of his belly.

Who were these two? Jordan wondered. They had to be from Randall's side of the family, because she certainly didn't recognize them as any of her kin.

"Nope, I believe we got the right door, girlie." The fat one with the gray ponytail wrapped a meaty hand around her arm, dragging her toward the door as the short guy held it open.

Something was terribly wrong here. The familiar smell of roses and gardenias permeated the church. The organ played a traditional ballad and ushers seated last-minute guests. All fairly normal. Yet this was no friendly stroll through the vestibule.

"Wait a minute," she commanded in the no-nonsense voice she used to get recalcitrant horses to obey.

"Sorry. Can't wait. No, siree. We got our orders." He continued to force-march her toward the doors.

"What orders?" His bulk was too much for her to handle. She tried to jerk her arm away, but his pudgy grip tightened, his sweaty fingers mangling the delicate, *expensive* fabric of her sleeve.

"Never you mind, little lady," he said.

She was used to dealing with headstrong males—four-legged ones. And Honor Bleu could be as stubborn as they came.

The difference was, Bleu would never intentionally hurt her. She couldn't be sure about this aging hippie or his rotund sidekick.

She needed help. Reinforcements.

"Daddy!" Jordan screamed, her high heels skidding against the hardwood floors, unable to find purchase, as she attempted to stop the momentum. Her veil fell from her fingers, landing in a heap with her purse.

"Here now. None of that. Just come peacefully, girlie, and everything will be fine."

"Not on your life, buster!" She screamed again, but the organ kept playing. Nobody came to her rescue. Where the hell was her father? Where was Randall? How could he not hear? Not know that she was in trouble? As her husband-to-be, wasn't he supposed to watch over her? Protect her?

And, by heaven, those were the thoughts of a wimp. She grabbed the door frame, trying to stop their progress. Her bouquet of ribbons and flowers slapped the wall and rained rose petals over the wood floor. From the corner of her eye, she saw Charity Arden round the corner.

"Oh, for pity's sake. Not again!" Charity said, reaching into the pockets of the fisherman's vest she wore over a gauzy pastel dress.

Now they were getting somewhere, Jordan thought. Charity Arden had a deadly accurate aim with film canisters. She'd proved as much just last week by felling the bandits at Kate Bingham's wedding.

"Stop right there, sister," the short guy said. "Just keep your mouth shut and nobody will get hurt."

Jordan's heart slammed against her chest as he whisked aside his jacket, showing the butt of a gun he had jammed into his cummerbund.

Charity's hand stilled, her eyes widening in surprise, and Jordan gave an understanding nod. At least the photographer had tried—which was more than could be said about anyone else around here. She had an idea she could scream down the house and the bridesmaids wouldn't budge from their makeup session at the mirror.

The sun nearly blinded her as the two men ushered her out the door. And she'd had enough.

Sounding low from a distance, a rumbling din gathered momentum, building to a deafening roar.

The distraction was just what she needed to break free. She jammed her spike heel into her captor's foot and simultaneously elbowed him in his overlarge belly. He let out a startled oomph and doubled over, lost his balance and toppled down the concrete steps like a fallen oak. The short guy, clearly astonished by the sight of a human bowling ball heading straight for him, sprang out of the way. The piece of paper clutched in his hand went sailing.

Jordan snagged it. She wanted to know who these clowns were.

The roaring in her ears did not subside. A motorcycle, she realized. Loud and lethal. Like a thundering mustang, it sprang forward, heading straight for them. Jordan stood her ground, wondering if she'd be forced into a dangerous game of chicken. Well, why the hell not? she thought in disgust, her heart hammering. What should have been the happiest day in her life had turned to ruin.

The motorcycle didn't show any signs of braking.

The bungling intruders scattered.

Jordan didn't budge.

Breaking every noise-abatement law in the county, the maniac on the bike cranked the front wheel at the last minute, executing an impressive power slide that halted mere inches from her feet.

Impressions flashed in her mind as recognition stole her voice. Hair nearly as long as hers. Masculinity so powerful her breath caught. A face so handsome it made her want to weep—or throw every bit of good reason she possessed right out the window.

Tanner Caldwell.

My God, it *had* been him last night.

"Get on, party girl."

Jordan hesitated, feeling paralyzed even though her heart raced at an unhealthy speed.

People were pouring out of the church doorway— at last.

Shorty was fumbling at his waist for his gun.

"You either take your chances with me or them."

His voice was low and rough, impatient. Yet his eyes were steady. Jordan was sure she was having some bizarre dream—either that or she'd fallen down the rabbit hole in a weird Alice-in-Wonderland reenactment.

But now was not the time for indecision. Something in Tanner's gaze, the barest flicker of softening, made up her mind. He was here. The closest. The wedding guests would never get to her in time.

She made a split-second decision. Faced with guns—the town was going to get a horrible reputation—and the lack of law enforcement to come to the rescue, Tanner was her best choice. For the moment.

Just until she had time to think more clearly.

With adrenaline pumping at a dizzying rate, she hoisted up her dress and flung her bedraggled flowers over her shoulder. The bouquet landed like a spiraling football in Charity Arden's hands.

Amid shouts and astonished expressions, Tanner Caldwell grabbed Jordan by the arm and swung her onto the back of his bike.

"For God's sake, keep that dress away from the wheels." He snatched a pair of aviator-style sunglasses from his shirt pocket, shoved them on and revved the engine.

With her spike heels hooked around the rungs of the foot pegs, and her dress pulled practically to her waist—showing off-white silk stockings and a good portion of her garter belt—Jordan clutched at Tanner's waist and held on for dear life.

The Harley vibrated beneath her and leaped forward like a feral beast, leaning into the curve as they barreled around Grape Street and raced past gaping guests in wedding attire.

In a blur of flashing scenery, she noticed Randall standing on the church steps, hands on hips, his blond hair styled and sprayed as if defying the June breeze to mess it up.

Her intended husband glanced around—for help? she wondered fleetingly. Or to see who was witnessing his bride taking off with another man? She felt the need to explain, started to tug at Tanner's shirt to get his attention, then realized that now was not a good time to stop and chat.

A sixties-model minibus pulled a U-turn on Walnut and took off in a squeal of tires—apparently in pursuit.

But why? What the heck was going on here?

Jordan tightened her arms around Tanner's waist. The wad of paper clenched in her fist was poking her palm. She straightened it as best she could and leaned around his shoulder to have a look.

Ransom.

The bold black letters had her heart slamming harder against her chest. Eyes tearing from the wind, she couldn't read the rest.

"Kidnapping?" she said incredulously, the whizzing air stealing the word from her.

Tanner took one hand off the handlebars. She felt his fingertips caress her palm, then felt him gently pry the paper from her numb hold. She spared a thought for their immediate safety when he took his eyes off the road long enough to scan the crude note before slipping it into his shirt pocket.

Who in the world would want to kidnap her? It was too much. Things like this didn't happen in Grazer's Corners. Well, she amended, maybe they did. This was the second week in a row that a wedding had been interrupted—in a bizarre manner!

She glanced back over her shoulder. The motorcycle wobbled.

She felt Tanner's chest rumble, and thought she heard him say, "Be still."

How did he expect her to be still and keep an eye on their pursuers at the same time?

"I think they're coming after us!" she shouted, feeling the whip of Tanner's long hair against her cheek. It was just like him to flout the law and not wear a helmet.

He turned his head, his lips practically brushing her forehead. "There's no way that bucket of bolts can catch this bike."

No. Judging from the blur of scenery zooming past, it was doubtful a full-blown race car would catch them.

With her head pounding—from a slight hangover and too much stimulation—she plastered herself against Tanner's back.

"Ease up, Blackie. Just relax and pretend you've got one of your fancy horses between your legs."

Blackie. The nickname sent a soft thrill through her, a thrill she should not be feeling on her wedding day—with a man who wasn't her groom.

But instead of easing up, her arms and thighs tightened around him. The way he was taking the curves, it was a wonder her feet didn't leave a trail of sparks on the asphalt. She felt out of control. At his mercy.

The image of the townspeople, and of Randall, watching in astonishment as they'd pulled away, was imprinted in her mind. What must they be thinking?

That bad-boy Tanner Caldwell had kidnapped her, that was what.

She finally peeled herself from his back long enough to have a look around. They were traveling north on U.S. 99 now, away from town.

"Where are we going?"

He didn't answer. The muscles of his forearm bunched as he cranked the throttle, increasing their speed. Hot dry air whipped past, billowing her dress. She snatched at the hem, holding it higher, crushing the delicate fabric. Thank goodness part of the dress was still tucked beneath her. Otherwise the virginal-white, G-string panties she'd bought and worn for Randall's eyes only, would be exposed for all the world to see.

As it was, the expanse of thigh between the tops of her silk stockings to nearly her panties was bared.

A bride on the back of a Harley with her dress hiked around her waist wasn't your everyday sight, and the picture they presented was creating a major stir with the truckers on 99. Air horns blared, men leered, and a family in a minivan looked scandalized.

Despite the circumstances and the incredible events of the morning, Jordan felt a bubble of laughter surface.

"Hell," Tanner muttered.

"What?"

A small farming town lined both sides of the freeway. He veered off at the next exit and wheeled into a convenience station, shutting off the Harley's engine. Jordan could feel the perspiration trickle between her breasts. Now that they were no longer moving, the heat was stifling.

And the rapid pumping of her heart was making her hotter.

"Why are we stopping here?" She cast a nervous glance toward the highway. No sight of the hippie and his sidekick.

Tanner got off the bike and gently steadied her until she was standing beside him. Reaching for the duffel bag tied to the bar behind the seat, he extracted a pair of jeans and a T-shirt.

"We've got to ditch that dress. We're likely to cause a pileup on the freeway."

"Ditch…"

He held out the clothes. She stared at them as though they were writhing, venomous snakes.

"Are you out of your mind? I'm not *ditching* this dress. I'll have you know it cost ten thousand dollars!"

"Pity. It's not worth it."

"I beg your pardon."

"It's just a bunch of fabric."

"And imported lace, beads and genuine pearls." Not that he'd know squat about high-class fashion.

He shrugged. "So it's an extravagant dress. Your old man's still overextending himself, I see."

"What would you know about our finances?" He'd hit a nerve with that comment. After all, her wedding day was mired hip-deep in her family's shaky finances.

"More than you'd expect. Go put these on before we draw a crowd." He tossed her the jeans and shirt.

She caught the garments and glanced toward the rest rooms by the side of the convenience store. Granted, she'd always been more comfortable in jeans, but the idea of wearing Tanner's clothes somehow seemed too...too personal.

"I don't think they'll fit. Besides, we can make it back to my house. It's not all that far."

"We're not going back to your house."

Her heart skipped a beat, then thudded with renewed vigor—right at her aching temples. This whole day was turning into a mess. "Why not?"

"Think about it, party girl. You saw the note. You've got gun-toting idiots trying to nab you off the church steps. You think they don't know where you live?"

She felt as though she were standing in a pit of quicksand...and sinking fast. "But why would anyone want to kidnap me?"

"I'd say that's what we need to find out."

"Us?"

"You got a better plan? Unless I've been misinformed, Grazer's Corners is a little short on law enforcement at the moment. And believe me, if they'll make a grab for you in broad daylight with a church full of people, they won't think twice about breaching a ranch where the closest neighbor is two miles away.''

What he said made sense. Still, she wasn't used to spur-of-the-moment decisions, to being out of control. She was supposed to be getting married. There were guests waiting. *Randall* was waiting.

''Daddy will take care of things.''

''Think so? Where was good old Maynard when you were screaming your lungs out?''

Jordan would like to know that, too. He should have been at her side, staying close so they could walk down the aisle. ''So what are you suggesting?''

''I'm suggesting we get out of town for a while until we get a handle on what's going down. And a bride on the back of a Harley is attracting way too much attention. Especially since we're being followed.''

Even though confusion battered her, she saw his logic. No sense in giving the would-be kidnappers an edge. There was no question they were as conspicuous as a giraffe on a pig farm.

Then she remembered an earlier thought. Tanner had come to her rescue; yet, to the town, it would surely appear as though *he* had kidnapped her.

So now they were both on the lam.

She fingered the buttery-soft denim. ''What will I do with my wedding dress?''

''Stuff it in my bag.''

That brought her head up and her temples pounded anew. ''I'm not stuffing this dress in a bag.'' The very thought offended her.

''Fine. Leave it here.''

She rolled her eyes. Men had no concept of the value of clothing. "I'll mail it home."

"Why don't you just leave a trail of bread crumbs for the kidnappers to follow while you're at it?"

Oh, this was too bizarre for words. Kidnappers, for heaven's sake. "Sarcasm is not necessary."

"Then get real. Use your head." He reached up and removed his sunglasses.

The power of that whiskey gaze nearly made her lose the thread of their conversation.

"Forgive me if my head is a little overwhelmed at the moment. It's not every day that people flash guns around and I go for a hair-raising ride with a motorcycle Romeo."

His brow lifted, his tone was soft and dark and dangerous. "Romeo? Is that how you see me?"

She hadn't meant to blurt that description. Damn it, her head was pounding and her brain just flat-out wasn't up to speed.

And she was *not* going to pick up the challenge she could see in his eyes.

"Do we plan to stay in this town?"

"No."

"Then it won't be like I'm announcing my whereabouts if I mail the dress home. There's a post office right over there."

"And there's a pawnshop," he countered, nodding toward the storefront with bars over its windows.

"Pawn it?"

"They'll hold it for thirty days. Plenty of time to get back and get it out of hock."

"I like my idea of mailing it better." She wondered if he had money on him to pay for postage.

Aside from the Harley—which he could have borrowed, for all she knew—he didn't appear to be particularly affluent. And at the moment, she was in the same boat. With her purse still at the church, she didn't have a cent to her name.

"We're wasting time, Blackie. You have exactly ten minutes to make a decision, change out of that dress and take care of any personal needs." He glanced at the gold watch at his wrist. "Starting now. If you're not done, I'll take you out of it myself."

Good Lord. The man had all but threatened her—improperly, at that—and here she stood, feeling soft, and achy and…thrilled.

"I don't think—"

"That's right, baby. *Don't* think. Just get a move on before that Woodstock relic makes up the distance I took great care to put between us."

She ought to demand that he take her home, ought to be seriously concerned that she was out of her mind for even considering sticking with him.

But she couldn't go back—not knowing what or *who* awaited her. And yet…

"Why, Tanner? Why are you helping me?"

He shrugged. "I got time on my hands."

His words were flippant, as if he didn't give a damn one way or the other. But for an instant, his gaze rested on her hair like the caress of a soft breeze, making a lie of his tough-guy terseness. That telling glimpse of the gentle man behind the mask confused her even more.

He was like a spirited stallion—gorgeous to look at, with steady brown eyes that could mesmerize, yet one wrong move, a careless disregarding of the rules, and the beast would emerge. She had to wonder if she was woman enough to handle a man like Tanner Caldwell, to find out what truly made him tick.

And she also had to wonder why she'd even think to try.

"A lot of people have time on their hands."

He glanced up at the clear blue sky. "Maybe I object to people taking away a person's freedom of choice. To brides being threatened by guns."

So did she—especially when *she* was the bride. Still, this being-on-the-run stuff was out of her realm of experience. As though he'd read her mind, his brow quirked.

"It's me or them, Blackie," he said softly. "What do you say?"

"Obviously I've chosen you or I wouldn't be standing here contemplating hocking my wedding dress."

"Smart move. Because I *am* your best bet. Trust me, I've got more experience in this sort of thing." He took her arm and ushered her across the street.

"I hope they have a phone in there."

"Forget it. No phone calls."

Her steps faltered. Had she jumped from the lifeboat into the bloodied shark-infested waters? "But I've got to find out what happened after we left. I've got to let somebody know—"

"Let's deal with one thing at a time. Like becoming a little less conspicuous."

Although she didn't care for his bossiness, he appeared to have her best interests in mind. And any minute now, that van decorated with peace symbols and garish flowers could show up.

Jordan had never been inside a pawnshop. Cramped and cluttered, it smelled musty and carried a little of everything, from a rack of cheap clothing to expensive guitars and flashy watches.

"See if you can find some clothes to fit," Tanner suggested. "I'll go talk to the owner."

With her head pounding in earnest, Jordan picked out a pair of plain-label jeans and a sleeveless denim shirt, then went into the small, dank dressing alcove protected by a threadbare curtain. She kept Tanner's clothes with her just in case these other "hand-me-downs" wouldn't do.

It was a tight fit in the cubicle, and she soon realized she had a major problem. Tiny, genuine cultured pearls formed a row of buttons down her back from her neck to her hips.

Her mother had helped her into the elaborate dress.

She'd counted on Randall to help her out of it.

On their wedding night.

Tonight.

And the man not five feet away on the other side of this dingy curtain was *not* her intended husband.

He was the stuff of her fantasies.

She clenched her fingers to keep them from trembling, felt herself growing hotter in the airless cubicle. How in the world was she supposed to undo thirty-three buttons? She debated for several minutes, staring at her reflection in the cloudy mirror. Her cheeks were flushed, her pupils dilated—from the dim interior, she told herself. Her body's reaction had nothing to do with her thoughts.

Thoughts of Tanner's fingers against her skin.

Last night she wouldn't have thought twice about flirting, daring him to put his hands on her.

Today was a different matter.

Nerves crowded in her throat. She reached back and made an awkward attempt at extracting the tiny pearls from their satin loops. Her elbows smacked the walls. Her upswept hair, loosened by the wild motorcycle ride, clung to her damp neck.

With her stomach twisted into knots of frustration, she managed all of two buttons, then gave up.

Turning, she stared at the moth-eaten curtain. He'd said ten minutes. She knew enough about Tanner Caldwell to know he was as good as his word. If he thought she was stalling, he wouldn't hesitate to come in after her.

Little did he know, she wasn't stalling. She was in trouble. Trouble with her thoughts, with her runaway hormones, and with this damned expensive wedding dress.

She was out of both time and options. Clenching her fist, she peeked around the edge of the curtain.

Tanner was leaning lazily against the wall, his eyes trained on the thin barrier that separated them. Their gazes locked. His brow rose.

He pushed off the wall and slowly crossed the store, his loose-hipped stride both casual and aggressive.

Her heart pounded harder.

"Something wrong, party girl?"

"I wish you'd stop calling me that."

He stared at her, his whiskey eyes giving away nothing.

She released a frustrated breath. "I...I can't get my dress undone."

A heartbeat of silence fell, heavy and expectant, in the stuffy pawnshop.

"Are you asking me to take your clothes off?" His voice was soft, taunting.

She nearly swooned at the look of blatant sexuality in his eyes. Shaking her head, disgusted by her fanciful imagination, she turned her back to him, snatching the hem of her dress out of the way. "Just undo me."

"My pleasure."

She felt his fingers at her neck, caressing. Her spine stiffened as involuntary chills chased down her arms, over her breasts, tightening her nipples.

"Relax. I'm not into audiences."

Oh, hell. She'd forgotten about the clerk. "Maybe you'd better come in here and close the curtain." She didn't bother to tell him she wasn't wearing a bra. He'd find out soon enough as it was.

"Two invitations in as many minutes. My lucky day."

He eased her forward, his fingers warm at her waist, and drew the curtain behind them. Within the confines of the cubicle, she felt his knees bump against the backs of her thighs.

Glancing at his reflection in the mirror, she tried to steady her breathing. If she didn't concentrate, she'd sound like Bleu after a flat-out run...all breathless and panting.

"Just do it."

He tsked. "Your groom might be into quickies, but I'm a man who likes to take my time."

"Oh, for pete's sake! We're not having sex. You're just helping me out of my dress."

"Better quit while you're ahead, party girl. Just

about everything that comes out of that sassy mouth is making me hot.''

Jordan closed her eyes and grabbed the walls for balance. She couldn't remember ever being this flustered.

Or excited.

What kind of woman was she to feel this way on her wedding day? With a virtual stranger, a man she hadn't laid eyes on in over ten years?

She heard the intake of his breath when he reached her mid-back, felt his fingers hesitate. Her gaze whipped to his, clinging to it in the mirror's reflection.

"No bra," he commented.

Defiance reared. It was her only defense against desire. An *inappropriate* desire.

"It *is* my wedding day," she reminded.

"Was." Expertly, he continued unthreading the pearls from their loops, his fingertips lingering.

Jordan had always thought she had an abundance of willpower. She was finding out right quick that she'd been misleading herself.

"Do you have to put your hands in my dress?"

"You want these buttons undone?"

"The buttons are on the outside."

"I'm no lady's maid, party girl. My fingers aren't designed for these dinky fastenings. Why the hell did you have so many put on?"

"The designer said it was subtly tantalizing."

"If it was my wedding night, I wouldn't be feeling subtle."

She didn't know what made her want to challenge him. "I thought you said you liked to go slow."

His eyes narrowed, and his lips formed into a

ghost of a smile. "Curious about my technique, are you?"

"In your dreams, ace."

He'd reached the final buttons at her hip. Deliberately, with his eyes holding hers in the cloudy reflection of the mirror, he traced the lower curve of her back.

Jordan jolted as though she'd been goosed with a branding iron. "I think I can handle it from here."

"Sure about that?"

"Positive."

"So prim," he murmured, stepping back, the curtain giving way as he did. "Last night's appearances to the contrary, breeding will tell."

"Don't start, Tanner."

"Too late. The line was drawn years ago. I'll say one thing for you, party girl. You've found your tongue."

"I told you to stop calling me that. And what do you mean by that remark?"

"Which one?"

"The tongue thing." Oh, that didn't sound at all right…or proper.

His hint of a smile reminded her of a dangerous predator about to pounce. "In school you were nervous as hell around me. You couldn't say two words without tripping all over yourself."

"That's because you were always so…" So what? she wondered, searching for the right word. *Sexy?* "So tough with a chip on your shoulder. Every time I tried to talk to you, you got that 'Touch-me-if-you-dare' look on your face and scared the daylights out of me."

She saw his handsome features go tight, saw the

emotion in his eyes retreat behind a mask. If she went in for fanciful thinking, she might imagine she'd seen hurt there, longing; a longing she herself had felt many times, yet had been unable to act upon.

Because according to the dictates of her bigoted social circle, Tanner Caldwell hadn't been good enough.

And her family had been instrumental in fostering that belief, had practically hand-placed that boulder-size chip on his shoulder.

She turned and reached out for him, not understanding why, but somehow knowing that right then, he needed to be touched.

But he stepped back, reverting to his enigmatic, bad-boy persona—the one that both dared and warned. The one that hid a multitude of emotions.

"Better hang on to that dress before I forget my manners...and my place."

His taunting smile was back now—the one, she realized, he used as a shield.

Jordan's breath actually hissed as she made a grab for the slipping shoulder seams of the gown. "I'm not trying to be provocative, which is more than I can say for you."

"That's right, baby. I'm bad. And don't you forget it."

He disappeared behind the curtain, leaving her trembling and off-balance.

Leaving her to wonder if she wouldn't have been better off taking her chances with the bungling kidnappers.

At the moment, she wasn't so sure Tanner was the lesser of two evils.

Chapter Three

Dressed in the jeans and sleeveless shirt, Jordan carefully gathered her wedding dress and went in search of the clerk. Since the pawnshop didn't have any shoes in her size, she wore her satin-trimmed pumps.

Tanner was standing guard by the front door, watching the streets. Good. She needed a few minutes to regroup before she went any more rounds of sexual innuendo with him.

Guns and jewelry took center stage in the glass display case above the counter. Trying to keep her dress from touching any contaminated surfaces, she kept it folded over her arm.

"I'd like to...um...pawn my dress for a while."

The clerk smiled, reminding her of a kindly grandfather—which seemed an odd association to make with a place like this. Jordan felt a twinge of guilt over her attitude toward the shop. It wasn't like her to judge outright. But she'd never been in an establishment such as this, wasn't sure how to act or what to expect.

"'For a while'?" the clerk questioned.

"Yes. Don't you have a policy to hold items for thirty days in case the seller changes her mind?"

"That's the policy. You and your intended having a lovers' spat?"

"He's not my intended." Not that she didn't wish he was. Stunned by the zinging thought that had sailed right out of nowhere, she clenched her fist round a wad of cool satin. For crying out loud, she had to stop thinking this way. "It's a long story. So tell me, how does this work?"

"You show me the merchandise, and I decide on a fair price."

She held up the gown.

"Not much call for wedding dresses around here. Not with the specialty boutique just down the road."

"I really don't want to sell it. But we're traveling by motorcycle and it's not feasible to wear the dress—"

"Jordan," Tanner interrupted softly. He came up behind her and gently placed his hand at her waist. She was so astonished by the change in him, she couldn't help but stare. One minute he acted like a tough guy, and the next he was sweet as all get-out. "I doubt that anyone's interested in our mode of travel."

"Oh." Stupid, she thought. They were on the run. And she'd been about to spill the details. She wasn't cut out for this cloak-and-dagger stuff. Longing, fierce and swift, welled in her. She wanted normality, wanted her horse beneath her, wanted to be riding into the wind through fields of wildflowers where she could blend in with the landscape, just be herself, not what everybody expected her to be.

"I'll give you fifty bucks for the dress."

That brought her head around and her temper boiling. "Fifty bucks! This is a ten-thousand-dollar dress!"

The man shrugged. "Not to me it isn't."

"But—"

"Fifty will be fine," Tanner said.

"No, it won't," she countered, drawing a breath to defend the yards of beautiful satin. "There're specially imported beads on this gown, intricate embroidery that took hours of labor to stitch." She'd tried to talk her mother out of buying the extravagant gown, knowing they couldn't afford it, but Daddy had insisted. Determined to save face, to avoid any hint that his financial empire was crumbling, he'd gone back to the bridal shop and purchased it himself. The sale was final, nonrefundable.

"I offered the duffel," Tanner reminded.

"It'll get ruined in your duffel. The thing's not even big enough to hold the train, let alone the whole dress."

"Then take the offer. It's not as though you're really selling it. You'll be back to get it."

Would she? At this point she felt bereft—without a safety zone to go back to or to head for. She had no idea who her enemy was. Reluctantly, she turned back to the clerk.

"Do you have a padded hanger and some plastic?"

"Let me check."

As the man disappeared into the back room, Tanner glanced out the front windows. "We need to get moving."

Jordan followed his gaze, nerves jumping again.

"Do you think they're on our trail?" There was

a phone at one end of the counter. A phone she desperately wanted to use. But whom would she call? And where? Would her family still be at the church? Organizing a search party, perhaps?

"Hard to say." He leaned an elbow on the counter, blocking her view of the phone. "I don't like taking chances, though."

"I assume you've got a plan?"

He nodded. "I've got a plan."

When he didn't say any more, she prodded. "Care to share it?"

"Not in here."

The clerk reappeared, holding a wire hanger, some tissue paper and a plastic zippered bag big enough to hold a body. She didn't even want to know what it had been used for. All she cared about at the moment was that it was roomy enough not to crush her dress.

Arranging the tissue herself over the wire hanger, she fussed with the dress, smoothing its folds into the bag just so. Satisfied, she handed it over and waited for payment.

The clerk passed her a five-dollar bill.

"I thought you said fifty."

"That's right. Minus thirty for the jeans and fifteen for the blouse."

Par for this increasingly horrendous day.

Jordan didn't bother with outrage this time. She simply took her five dollars and allowed Tanner to usher her outdoors where the fresh air was more than welcome after the stuffy interior of the pawnshop.

"What do you bet he charges me double to get

the dress back.'' She stuffed the claim-check receipt into her pocket.

''Probably more than double,'' Tanner said, swinging his leg over the Harley, then giving her a helping hand as she climbed on the back.

''We really should have held out for more money. My bargaining instincts are smarting.''

''It's all relative, Blackie. If he gave you more money, it'd just cost you that much more to get it back.''

''Yeah, well, my pride would feel a whole lot better.''

She wrapped her arms around his waist, feeling the muscles of his stomach tighten.

''*Now* what's the matter?'' she asked. His body language fairly shouted that she had cooties. She had a pressing, unladylike urge to hit something.

He shook his head and shoved on his sunglasses. ''It's gonna be a long ride.''

His tone said so much more than his words. That was when she realized that her unbound breasts were mashed solidly against him. She eased her hold.

''I'll make a deal with you.''

He booted the gearshift, but kept the clutch pulled in. ''I'm listening,'' he said tightly.

''As long as you're not going hell-bent for leather, I'll give you plenty of breathing room. You start scraping my toes on the pavement again and you're on your own. Braless or not, I'll stick to you like flypaper.''

''*Definitely* found your tongue,'' he muttered and eased the clutch out, the powerful motorcycle sounding a lot meaner than it acted.

Tanner wasn't sure if he would make it. Although

she was holding up her end of the bargain—giving him breathing room—each bump in the road shifted those enticing breasts against his back. Even with the wind whipping past, he could smell her scent. Something expensive, delicate. He resisted the urge to lift his fingers to his nose—the fingers that had touched her—to inhale the feminine smell he knew still lingered.

Her hands rested lightly at his waist and the warmth of her thighs cupped his hips. It was all he could do to keep the bike on the road and remember which turn to make.

He felt the soft slap of her hair tangling with his as she turned her head, watching the scenery. When they passed within spitting distance of Grazer's Corners, he felt her thighs tighten. Other than that slight flex, she didn't bug him about their destination.

Tanner appreciated that in a woman—quiet acceptance.

God knew he hadn't garnered much of it in his life.

"Poor white trash" was a label that didn't lend itself to respect.

He felt the familiar roil of emotions twist in his gut. Coming back to Grazer's Corners brought it all back to him—the shame, the desperation to get out, to *be* someone. He'd sworn he wouldn't come back.

Yet here he was, with his emotions tied in knots and his neck on the line for Jordan Grazer.

When he'd laid eyes on her in that wedding dress, he'd thought he'd died and gone to heaven, been granted every one of his secret dreams. How many times had he pictured her just like that, dressed in flowing white, looking at him as though he were her savior and her heart's desire all rolled into one rough package.

His jaw clenched as he reminded himself of one very important detail.

She'd been wearing that dress for another man.

An acceptable man. A fancy banker. A guy born into the right family who golfed at the country club and drank martinis with the upper crust.

A far cry from somebody like him who'd clawed his way out of poverty with a mix of street smarts and fists.

His fingers clenched around the throttle grip. The bike poured on speed.

And Jordan pressed her chest firmly against his back.

Ah, hell. He eased off; so did she.

But reprieve wasn't in the cards. He felt her fingers in his hair and jolted, nearly sending them into the ditch.

"Don't wreck us," she said in his ear.

"Then get your hands out of my hair."

"It's flying in my face."

He fished in his pocket, careful not to lose the ransom note, and pulled out a thin strip of leather.

Jordan snagged the leather band. "Keep your hands on the controls. I'll fix your hair." She felt his spine go rigid, saw a muscle tighten in his square jaw. She didn't know what he was so uptight about. Oh, it was obvious he was responding to the press of their bodies, but doggone it, so was she.

With the vibration of the motorcycle between her legs and six-foot-plus of hot male pressed against her, she was having a full range of erotic fantasies.

Dear God, both her brain and her hormones were on overload.

It was the day, she told herself. Wedding days meant wedding nights, which added up to sex.

And like a record stuck in a groove, each bump, look or caress sang out "Sex." Over and over.

But the groom in the starring role wasn't wearing a tux, nor did he have wheat-blond, perfectly styled hair.

No, the man creating such carnal, uncharacteristic thoughts wore jeans and boots and a look of hot sin.

Her fingers trembling, her knees tightening against his hips for balance, she tied his long hair into a ponytail, struck by the extreme intimacy of the act. She really needed to take herself in hand. All this fluttering and heart jumping was ridiculous. Jordan decided she was simply overwrought by the bizarre circumstances of the day. That was the only excuse she could come up with for the way her mind and body insisted on turning everything into some sort of sexual act.

Because she desperately wanted to linger over the feel of his hair in her hands, she curled her fingers into her palms and placed them on her knees, divorcing herself from turbulent fantasies of Tanner Caldwell.

The land was drenched in sunshine. Golden-brown pastures gradually gave way to a rolling landscape as the Harley ate up the miles. To the east, the Sierra Nevada created a magnificent backdrop to the cobalt sky, their distant peaks iced with lingering snow.

The road became curvy now, shaded by grand California oaks that had stood watch over the countryside for hundreds of years. Jordan eased her hands to Tanner's waist for balance as the motorcycle slowed, cutting off onto an unmarked road camouflaged by towering pines.

They'd spent nearly two hours traveling in a wide circle and had ended up only about half an hour from Grazer's Corners.

Yet the sight before her was like something from another world. A house of stucco and glass stood in isolated splendor on the shore of a freshwater lake. Stubborn wildflowers, confused by the lateness of the season, pushed their happy faces through blades of patchy grass that gave way to a meadow-like landscape.

When Tanner shut off the deep rumble of the Harley's engine, the land was hushed, save for the breeze whispering through the treetops and birds twittering to their mates. As though it had lost its way from the ocean, a gull winged over the mirror-still surface of the water, its white breast a stark contrast to the deep blue lake, its cries echoing off the majestic crags on the opposite bank.

Only lingering exhaust fumes from the motorcycle marred the sweet, clean scent of vegetation and cool water.

"It's beautiful," Jordan said, hiking a leg over the seat of the Harley before Tanner could assist her. The heels of her satin pumps sank into the loamy soil and if Tanner's hand hadn't shot out to steady her, she would have landed on her face when she tried to take a step.

"You're going to break your neck in those spikes."

She smiled. "In case you hadn't noticed, I'm a little short on footwear selections."

"Guess we'll have to expand your wardrobe."

Before she realized what he was about, he'd squatted in front of her. As if he were checking a horse's hoof for stones, he gripped her ankle and lifted her foot. Off-balance, she grabbed his shoulders, stunned when he snapped off the heel of her shoe.

"What in the world?"

He stared up at her, a strand of dark hair escaping the impromptu ponytail she'd fashioned. "Now the other one."

Lost in those mesmerizing whiskey eyes, she automatically shifted her weight and stood like a docile filly as he deliberately ruined her bridal pumps.

He was kneeling before her, much the way a groom would do while taking off his bride's garter.

Under her jeans was that article. Blue satin trimmed with white lace. But there was no gathering of single men waiting for the sexy item to be tossed—to determine who would dance with the lucky recipient who'd caught the wedding bouquet.

Dear Lord, Charity Arden had caught the bouquet. And under scary circumstances. Jordan hoped there wasn't a bad omen in that. Charity deserved better.

And thinking about wedding rituals sent worries tumbling through her mind. She couldn't help but consider the waste—the endless wedding preparations, the money spent on deposits, caterers, flowers, nets of birdseed, an elaborate champagne fountain, the multitiered cake decorated in white-on-white with strategically placed, fresh-cut orchids. So many details, from extravagant to simple, amounting to a small fortune.

A fortune gone down the drain. Funds her father couldn't afford to lose. He'd lost too much already.

And what of the friends and family who'd plunked down good money on gifts? Rearranged their schedules in order to attend what should have been a special day—particularly those who'd come from out of town?

And my God, she'd pawned her wedding dress, sealing any hope of salvaging the day.

The list of zingers appeared endless, each sending a stinging dart to her midsection. In mere minutes, everything familiar about her life had been snatched away.

Had she subconsciously started the downfall last night? Had she wanted freedom so badly, a walk on the wild side, so desperately that she'd sacrificed everything and everybody to get it?

Worry escalated, running rampant, making her dizzy.

What if someone at Gatlin's had recognized her, overheard her plans with Charity and decided to cash in?

Tanner touched her cheek and she jumped, having forgotten for the moment that he was even there.

"You okay?" he asked.

"I shouldn't be here." Her gaze clung to him, pleading for validation, for reassurance. "Did I make a mistake? Leaving that way?"

His shoulders lifted. "The guy had a gun, Jordan." He patted his breast pocket where the ransom note lay. "Greed makes a man reckless…and determined."

"Maybe Randall and some of the other men could have tackled them."

Tanner snorted, letting her know his opinion on that front.

Jordan felt disloyal because a part of her agreed with him. Randall wasn't the type of man to initiate or participate in confrontations. The extent of his muscle flexing was at the country-club gym with a forty-pound barbell. Even when she'd ridden off with Tanner, her intended husband hadn't taken the first step off the church threshold to give chase.

Still, she felt honor-bound to defend her groom. "They were kind of far away, I suppose."

He didn't challenge her excuse. "It's probably just as well. In a crowd that size, a stray bullet can turn into tragedy."

Eerie chills tracked down her spine, and she looked toward the lake, staring at the powerboat bumping gently against the wooden dock. It was tragic enough that she'd agreed to give her hand in marriage, made a promise that she'd longed to run from.

A loss of lives because of her—even indirectly— would have been devastating.

Tanner had mounted the porch and was in the process of trying various keys in the lock. In an effort to calm herself, Jordan drew in a breath of sweet, June air, then joined him there, tamping down a twinge of unease about their isolation.

Any minute now, the enormity of the day was bound to close in on her. In the meantime, she fought the suffocation, the uncertainty, trying desperately to look on the events as an adventure.

"You've probably got an unjust kidnapping

charge hanging over your head," she commented when he jammed the fourth key into the lock. "Are we about to add breaking and entering to the list?"

"Just when I think you're a fairly down-to-earth chick, you go into that deb talk."

That stung. "I was kidding." Didn't the man have a sense of humor?

"Yeah," he said as the door swung open. "So was I."

"Oh." She was having trouble reading him. Nerves, probably.

The inside of the house lived up to the exterior's promise. Understated elegance, she noted, with a breathtaking wall of glass that looked out on the serene lake.

She moved to stand by the windows, feeling the noonday sun penetrate the panes, warming her.

"Are there neighbors?"

"Not for several miles. It's unlikely anyone will find you here."

A statement like that should have made her nervous. After all, Tanner was a virtual stranger, a man she hadn't seen since they were both teens.

A bad-boy misfit from the wrong side of the tracks.

But against all reason, she wasn't concerned about her safety with Tanner.

The sexual tension fairly screaming between them was another matter altogether. It made even small talk difficult.

With her back to the room, she saw his reflection in the panes of the window as he prowled the space, checking the corners and furnishings as though he expected kidnappers to jump out toting Uzis.

She turned then, allowed herself the pleasure of watching him move. He was over six feet tall and had the fluid grace some men were born with—a presence that both intrigued and thrilled.

And they were alone.

Oh, dear God. It was catching up with her. Was she being naive to put her trust in Tanner Caldwell? It seemed a little fishy—awfully convenient that he'd shown up in town around the same time somebody attempted to nab her. She shouldn't be here. Maybe the guests were still at the church. Maybe…

"I've made a mistake," she said wildly. "I should go back. Everybody's counting on me. I've let them down—Randall, my family." Words poured out without order. "My horses. There won't be anyone to take care of them."

He was in front of her in an instant, his handsome features concerned, his fingertips gentle against her cheek.

"Hey, it'll be okay."

"How? Somebody wants to kidnap me, I've skipped out on my wedding—"

"Not intentionally," he reminded her.

"That doesn't matter. I gave my word. Everyone's counting on me," she repeated.

Tanner frowned. Those weren't the words of an excited bride. "Who's counting on you, Blackie?"

She shook her head and stepped away, turning back toward the wall of windows. His fingers curled into a fist. He shouldn't crave the touch of this woman's skin. Shouldn't want to take her in his arms and soothe her worries.

She belonged to another man. A wimp, to be sure, but that was beside the point.

He saw her press her thumb and forefinger to her temple. The desire to touch her again won. He'd thought he had more sense than to beat his head against the wall. Evidently, he didn't.

He stepped behind her, put his hands on her tense shoulders. She jumped, then settled down.

"Headache?" he asked softly.

"A slight one."

"I bet you didn't eat this morning."

A shudder worked through her body. She shook her head. "Wedding jitters."

"And a little bit of a hangover, party girl?"

In the reflection of the glass, he saw her gaze snap to his. He tried to keep the smirk from his lips and his voice, and continued to massage. "Surprised the hell out of me to see you at Gatlin's last night."

"I like the place," she said.

"You've never been there before." He knew a bluff when he heard it.

"How…?" Her shoulders relaxed a little more. "Okay, so it was only my second time. But it's a fun, down-to-earth place."

"Like a bachelorette party for one? I couldn't help but notice you didn't have any bridesmaids in tow."

She chuckled. "Heaven forbid."

"Not country club enough for your friends?"

"That sounds really snooty, Tanner."

"Most of your friends *are* snooty."

She glanced over her shoulder at him. "You haven't laid eyes on me in ten years. What would you know about my friends?"

"Nothing much changes in Grazer's Corners.

Simple deduction.'' He wasn't going to admit he'd kept tabs on her over the years. ''You hungry?''

''Not really. It seems like my jitters have switched gears. I don't think I could eat.''

''Might help the headache.'' He dropped his hands and stepped back, knowing he had no business touching her. It made him want to do more.

''Is there even food in this house?''

''The essentials. Beer, milk, cereal. Probably frozen stuff in the deep freeze.''

''You've been staying here?''

''For a couple of days.''

''I'd never have known it from the way you fumbled with the keys.''

''They all look alike.''

''A dab of nail polish will take care of that.''

''I'm fresh out of finger paint.''

She smiled softly. ''Do you come here often?''

''Not often. It's a little closer to Grazer's Corners than I'd like.'' He saw her eyes go all soft and concerned, remembered how she'd always been one to champion the underdog. By damn, he didn't want her thinking of him in those terms.

With his jaw tight, he strode into the kitchen. He knew the exact minute she followed him. Even though she hadn't yet said a word, he *felt* her presence.

''Speaking of Grazer's Corners, you said you had a plan.''

He nodded.

''Well, don't keep it to yourself. We're alone now.''

Yeah, and it was driving him crazy. ''I've got a friend I can call. He'll send somebody to town to snoop around, let us know what we're dealing with.''

"I feel like I should be doing that myself.''

"Since you're the target, that doesn't seem like the wisest avenue.'' He opened the double doors of the refrigerator. The carton of milk and six-pack of beer looked pitiful in the vast interior.

"I could get a gun.''

His head whipped around and he leveled her with a scowl that should have had her backing up. Hell, he could see his own eyebrows. "Would you use it?''

Her breath hissed out. "No.''

Some of his tension eased. "That's one of the first things you learn about guns. Never threaten unless you're positive you've got the guts to follow through. Otherwise the perp will take it away and use it on you.''

"You sound as though you know what you're talking about. Do you carry a gun?''

He went back to inspecting the contents of the fridge. Nothing gourmet had materialized since the last time he'd checked. "I have a permit.''

"Are you in law enforcement?''

"Security.'' Frozen bread and lunch meat. With the defrosting aid of the microwave, they'd have to make do. "I've done some bodyguarding.''

"But you don't anymore?''

He placed their lunch selection on the counter, crossed his arms over his chest and leaned against the tile.

"Looks like I am now.'' And it wasn't tough to guard a body like Jordan's.

She caught him staring at her. Their gazes met,

locked. He saw the nervous sweep of her tongue. She was a gutsy lady, but she was just a little scared of him. Perhaps that was an advantage. He didn't have any business getting close.

And he didn't go in for scaring women. That was a sure way to have him keep his distance.

Her chest rose as she drew in a breath. "So. You'll call your friend to investigate. Then what?"

"Then we sit tight and wait for news."

"But what about my wedding?"

"Guess it's postponed." His shrug was flippant. The roiling in his gut was far from it. "Better the kidnapper you know…"

Chapter Four

Jordan grabbed the back of a chair and sat down before her knees gave out. The implications of that statement had her mind going off on another tangent.

It was probably just the events of the day, she thought, staring at his broad back. The ponytail she'd fashioned was coming loose, several strands falling across his shoulders.

She shouldn't be creating lurid fantasies over felony offenses. This was serious. Scary. Somehow, though, she kept losing sight of her dilemma.

Once she was fairly sure her voice wouldn't tremble, she spoke.

"It's not as though *you* kidnapped me."

He shrugged, popped some bread into the microwave. "Looked that way to the town. Chances are, your old man recognized me. He's never been one to give me the benefit of the doubt."

"I'm sorry."

"Not your problem."

But she took it on anyway. From habit. "Daddy can be judgmental. Deep down he's not all bad."

"I admire your loyalty."

"There's no need to be sarcastic."

He gave her a steady look. "I meant it as a compliment. Loyalty was always one of your nice qualities."

"Oh. Thank you."

"Now don't go all tongue-tied on me again."

Her shoulders squared. "I'm not tongue-tied. I hadn't expected compliments from you."

"Why? You should get plenty. All that black hair, those moss-green eyes...a body built for sin. Hell, baby, you've got a face guaranteed to stop male traffic. I imagine you walk down the street and guys forget to watch where they're going—end up wrecking their shiny cars. Probably keeps the insurance agents in town busy."

She wasn't sure whether to be insulted or pleased. "I can turn that around on you, Tanner. How do you like being labeled a beefcake pinup?"

"You assigning that label to me?"

Caught in her own trap. Never mind that he'd make a nun rethink her vows. Jordan was far from a nun. And staring at those masculine features, all that flowing hair, that tough body... Well, it was sending her brain into way too many flights of fancy.

She glanced at the package of frozen lunch meat he held in his hand. "Do you want some help with that?"

"You know how?"

"Don't be a smart aleck."

"It's a legitimate question, duchess. Your family employs a cook."

"You must really think I'm a spoiled brat." Duchess, Blackie, baby. Couldn't the man just use her name?

He turned and slid the meat into the microwave. "Sorry. Sometimes I'm not fit for polite company."

She opened her mouth to take issue. He held up a hand.

"That wasn't a dig at you. I really was speaking of myself."

She wondered what made the anger simmer so close to the surface, wondered what made him tick. Even in school he'd kept her at arm's length. He'd been such a loner, and she'd felt sorry for him...and intrigued. But even when she'd tried to approach him, he'd fired off something shocking, usually a challenge. And for the life of her, she'd never been able to rise to the dare of his thrilling taunts.

She'd only been able to dream. Alone in her bed, she'd thought about him. Grooming the horses, she'd imagined him helping her. Riding through the hills, she'd wished he'd been there to share with her, to laugh with her.

Dreams... She'd had plenty of them.

Dreams that would have horrified her family.

Tanner was right in that respect. Daddy would never have given him the benefit of the doubt, would never have considered him good enough to sit at their dinner table.

Not that Tanner would have accepted such an invitation.

He had more pride than any man she knew.

He placed a ham sandwich in front of her. "Beer or ice water?"

"Ice water." She wouldn't take a chance on alcohol muddling her thoughts. She was sluggish enough as it was. "I'll get it."

"I'm up. Stay put."

This wasn't going to work, she decided. Too many conflicting emotions were at war inside her. He made her feel like the duchess he'd called her. And contrary to what he thought, she wasn't used to people waiting on her.

She was used to doing things herself. That way, she knew they'd get done. Rarely did she leave anything to fate or chance.

Which was why she should have been at the church getting married.

Her marriage would guarantee the loan her family needed.

Tanner sat down across from her and dug into his sandwich like a man who hadn't eaten in a week. Jordan just picked at hers. Her stomach was jumpy and her mind was too busy.

"You're not eating."

She took a bite just to make him happy. "I keep thinking about all the catered food at the reception. I hope the guests won't let it go to waste."

"Probably won't. People come to weddings to eat."

"And to see a couple get married," she inserted.

He laid down his sandwich—what was left of it. "Any idea who those goons were? Did you recognize them?"

"No. When they came in the side doors, I thought they were people from Randall's side of the family. I figured they'd just gone in the wrong door."

"No." He took a swig of beer. "It was deliberate."

She flashed on a thought, worried over it for a moment. "How was it that you happened to be there?" Obviously she was more stressed than she'd realized. She should have asked that question sooner.

"A hunch."

"Why in the world would you have a hunch that somebody would try to kidnap me?"

"Heard 'em talking about it last night at Gatlin's."

Nausea welled, pounding through her. "Oh, no. I *did* cause this."

Tanner frowned. He didn't like the look of distress that came over her smooth features. "What are you talking about?"

"I shouldn't have gone. I just wanted one night. Something different. I shouldn't have flouted convention on the eve of my wedding." She rubbed her temples. "I didn't think anyone would recognize me."

"You're thinking the plot was hatched on the spur of the moment?" Tanner, for one, was extremely glad she'd gone. That dressed-for-sin outfit had given him a sleepless night, but he wouldn't have wanted to miss it. Or the sexy, sultry dance, the confidence. The woman was dynamite. And hell on the nerves. But obviously still suffering from a headache.

"What other explanation is there?" she asked.

"Several. But that's not one of them." He got up and rummaged through the cupboards. "I heard them talking in the parking lot. This was planned—poorly, to be sure. But it wasn't spur-of-the-moment. Here, take these." He shook a couple of pain relievers into his palm, held it out.

She accepted the tablets. "The way I'm feeling, it'll take something a lot stronger."

He told himself he wouldn't touch her. Though his body went rigid from the effort to resist, his feet moved of their own accord, his hands automatically reaching for her temples.

He was burning to ask what exactly she'd wanted last night. *"One night,"* she'd said. *"Something different."* His mind supplied myriad answers—all of them slanted toward the carnal.

Standing behind her chair, he pulled her head back to rest against his chest, his fingers diving into her mass of hair, kneading her scalp. A couple of hairpins scattered.

She tried to pull away. He held her steady. "Relax. I'm just giving the medicine a little help."

Jordan wasn't certain she could comply. She was an only child and her parents weren't the demonstrative type. She couldn't remember the last time someone had ministered to her this way—unless she'd paid them.

It took everything in her to keep from purring...or drooling. His touch was heaven.

She might have imagined the restraint she felt in his touch, but at the moment, she couldn't work up the energy to give it adequate thought.

His fingertips moved to her temples, her closed eyelids, her hairline. She felt him hesitate, hovering as though weighing a decision.

She opened her eyes. Looked up.

With her head tilted back, resting against his stomach, she gazed at him. And he was staring back.

The fire in those whiskey-colored eyes made her heart pound, made her forget all about her headache. Mouth dry, she could not look away.

Did his head move closer?

The moment spun out like a videotape put on freeze-frame. Her lips parted. *Just once,* she thought. How many times had she imagined how that sensual mouth would feel against hers? Had ached for the feel of it.

Without thought, she reached up, covered his hand.

And waited.

The back of her head pressed against his firm belly. *Yes. Just bend down.*

He stepped back so fast she nearly got whiplash. "So, what were the big honeymoon plans?"

Jordan was mortified. He probably thought she was sex starved, looking at him all moon-eyed. And really, what did she expect? After her performance last night, and now… Well, she'd definitely given him the wrong impression. This was no way for a woman to act on her wedding day—at least, not with a man other than her groom.

Now, not only would Tanner think she was spoiled, he'd think she was a shallow runaround to boot.

Nothing could be further from the truth, but the damage was already done.

She stood and took their dishes to the sink. "Randall had some business deals pending, so we were only going to take a few days and drive over to Big Sur."

"A few days? Pity. Thought the man had better sense."

She glanced at him sharply. "I'll take that as a compliment."

"As it was meant."

His expression gave away nothing. Still, when he

moved to help her with the dishes, she waved him back. She didn't trust herself not to climb right up his body. Yes, Tanner was a man who'd want a *much* longer honeymoon.

And she *wasn't* going to spend time on that image just now.

"I think I can handle a couple of plates and glasses."

"Suit yourself." Ankles crossed, he leaned against the counter, watching her.

Making her nervous.

Jordan racked her brain for conversation. She didn't want to talk about Randall. Those reckless, restless feelings were welling again; the yearning for freedom—to start something she wasn't free to start.

With Tanner Caldwell.

She cleared her throat. "Who owns this house?"

"A raven-haired Goldilocks," he murmured, and she thought he was ignoring the question. His penetrating gaze rested on her hair, slowly moved downward. "We've already settled in and helped ourselves to the porridge, and you're just now getting around to asking about the owners?"

By any other man, that blatant visual inspection would have been insulting. From Tanner, it had the power to set her terribly off-balance.

"You ate," she reminded. "I didn't." Dear Lord, she wished he wouldn't look at her that way.

"Mr. B. would be offended. He'd think you were refusing his hospitality."

"Mr. B.?"

"Samuel Bartholomew. A man I worked for. It's his house."

"Oh. Your boss." Relief that their hideaway was

owned by a *male* friend rather than a female was greater than it should have been. "It's nice of him to let you use the place."

Tanner noted that she'd misunderstood—she'd thought he'd used the present instead of the past tense. For some reason, he decided not to correct her assumption that Mr. B. was still his employer.

He also noticed that she was nervous as hell. The way her gaze kept darting toward him, then skittering away, and the fine trembling in her fingers that she tried to hide beneath the soapy water, was making it hard to concentrate.

It was making him hard, period.

"Mr. B.'s the most generous man I know."

"Will he be joining us?"

"No. This is just a getaway place for him."

"And you use it sometimes?"

"Sometimes." When the longing became a gnawing in his gut and he just needed to be close. To catch a glimpse of a dark-haired beauty who'd stuck in his mind and heart like the chorus of a favorite song, popping up, reverberating around and around until he could think of nothing else.

And when that happened, nothing helped. Not work or other women or the dangerous speed of the Harley on a wide-open road.

Those were the times when he came here. When he tortured himself even more by being so close— a mere half-hour drive from Grazer's Corners—especially knowing he couldn't make a move to seek her out, to touch her...to hope.

The episodes didn't happen often. The agony of wanting this woman and being unable to have her was enough to last for a good long while.

So he'd kept himself busy, determined to make his security business—and his name—so successful, no one would ever dare to close a door in his face again.

And he'd done that, in spades; become a force to be reckoned with. Hell, he could buy that fancy country club Grazer's Corners was so proud of and not even make a dent in his bank account.

But his pride was a lot bigger than he'd thought. He didn't want to win Jordan by default. He wanted her to care. About him, the man. So he kept his mouth shut and let her think he was still the same old Tanner Caldwell, merely eking out a living on a scale one would expect of a high-school dropout from the wrong side of the tracks.

When the glassware was in danger of being worn away by the running water, he reached over and shut off the tap, then passed her a dish towel.

He noticed the faraway look in her eyes and jammed his hands in his pockets to keep from reaching out to soothe.

"How long do you think I'll need to stay here?" she asked.

"Could be a day or a week. Depends on what we can find out."

"I'm worried about my horses."

"Didn't you make arrangements for someone to take over while you were honeymooning?"

She shrugged. "I told you, we'd only planned to be gone a couple of days. Daddy was going to take care of feeding them. But they need exercise."

"You don't have stable hands?"

"I've got a blacksmith and a vet. And a part-time trainer who helps out. I told him to take a vacation."

"Why? Seems you'd need him there more than ever while you're gone."

"I don't trust anyone with Bleu when I'm not around."

"Bleu?"

"My stallion."

He hid a smile. "Haven't learned the art of delegating, hmm?"

"Oh, I know how. I just choose not to do it. Experience has taught me that no one cares the way I do. If one of the horses comes up with swollen fetlocks, I'll make sure he's all the way healed before he's run. Outsiders aren't as patient. They get around champions and can't resist seeing what they're made of."

He frowned at the fierceness of her tone. "You've had a handler damage one of your horses?"

"More than damage." She twisted the dish towel into a knot. "The mare died."

"Oh, man. That's tough."

"It was. Dawn's Lady had special needs. The vet said her dying was inevitable, but I don't believe it. They called it 'sudden death syndrome.'"

Jordan shook her head, the memory still sharp and stinging, even after all these years. "She had a slight heart irregularity, but we were controlling it. Until a flunky stable hand with too much testosterone and not enough brains got some wild idea that it'd be okay to run her flat out. Granted, in her day, Dawn's Lady was a prizewinner, from Saratoga to the Kentucky Derby. But she wasn't strong enough for that vigorous pace anymore."

She folded her arms around her waist. "When I found her lying in the stall I thought she was asleep.'' Her tone softened with raw emotion. ''But she was gone. Since then, I'm very territorial about my horses and stables.''

''That's a big responsibility to take on alone. Especially with the work you do in your father's offices.''

Surprise stole her voice for a moment. ''How did you know I work there?''

Where before his gaze had been steady, now it shied away. He looked as though he'd like to snatch the words back.

''Somebody once mentioned it,'' he said. ''I assumed you were still at it.''

Jordan wondered if he'd been keeping tabs on her. But why? She dismissed the notion as wishful thinking. ''Part-time, yes. But my main income comes from the board of other people's horses. Someday the breeding's going to pay off, though. Bleu has top-notch bloodlines. He'll sire winners.'' She stopped, realizing she'd gotten wound up about her favorite subject. Tanner looked interested enough— his eyes weren't glazed over in boredom like Randall's had a tendency to do when she waxed on about her animals—but she felt like a chatterbox.

''Sorry, I get carried away when it comes to my horses.''

''No need to apologize. I like horses. Mr. B.'s got an impressive stable. The two of you would get along great.''

''Really?''

''Yeah. How about Russell—''

''Randall.''

''Whatever. He share your love of champions?''

She rolled her eyes. "From a distance. He's allergic to anything with fur."

His dark brow arched. "A statement like that gets me to wondering, Blackie."

"About what?"

"Why you'd want to hitch up with a guy who doesn't share your interests, your goals."

She tried not to flinch, tried to push the doubts to the back of her mind. She'd made a promise, and once given, her word was gold.

Besides, Randall was a respected man in the community. When every other financial institution around refused even to consider her father's loan application, Randall had come through.

Or would come through.

Once they were married, once their family names were linked, the powers that be would see the paperwork in a different light.

And her father was desperately counting on that loan. If he didn't get his hands on a sizable chunk of money soon, they'd lose the estate—and her stables along with it.

After all Maynard had done for her over the years, had given her, she owed him more than a slap in the face.

She owed it to him to keep her promise.

To marry Randall.

As usual, a weight of dread settled in her stomach. Oh, she cared for her fiancé, but there was a spark missing, a fire she'd always thought she'd feel toward the man she chose to wake up beside every morning for the rest of her life.

And sharing, she realized, her brows pulling together. She was happiest when mucking out a stall or hosing down a well-exercised horse. Randall hated to get his hands dirty.

But he had other qualities, she told herself. He treated her like a lady, had a great laugh, was attentive. And he was in love with her—not just her name.

It aggravated her that she'd allowed Tanner to stir up her doubts.

She shoved her hair off her face, deciding she was simply overwrought. Understandable after being manhandled and nearly snatched off the church steps by two strangers.

"Randall's a good man."

"There's a saying about the character of people who don't like animals."

"I never said he didn't like animals," she defended. "He's allergic to them. That's not something he's chosen."

"Just an observation, duchess. No need to get snippy."

"You'd be snippy, too, if you were worried sick over a church full of disappointed guests and a stable of horses depending on someone for care—"

"And a bridegroom left in the dark," he reminded.

She squared her shoulders, met the amused sparkle in his ginger eyes, tossed the challenge right back at him. "I'd have gotten to that if you hadn't interrupted."

He shook his head and took the dish towel from her hands before she ended up shredding the thing. "I could almost feel sorry for good old Randall."

When he left it at that, she curled her fingers into her palms, feeling bereft without something to hold on to. Reaching for Tanner wasn't an option. "I'm sure you intend to clarify that—because I assure you, Randall isn't a man who inspires pity."

"He does when he's third or lower on your list of worries."

"Oh, this is ridiculous. Of course, he's my main concern." She'd have to stay on her toes around Tanner Caldwell. This bad boy with long hair and killer dimples didn't miss a thing. "He's probably beside himself wondering what's going on. I imagine he's already contacted the FBI."

"I think there's a twenty-four-hour delay before they'll get involved."

"Not when there were witnesses."

"You got on my bike of your own free will, Blackie. Besides, I didn't hear any talk of the feds being called in to look for Katie."

The way he said Kate's name made her pause. "Did you know Kate Bingham?"

"In school. She was a year ahead of me. Always focused and determined, a five-foot-two dynamo. I bet she makes a hell of a principal. Little surprised about the sheriff title, though."

"You've learned an awful lot for just breezing into town." There was no call for her to feel the zing of jealousy. Kate was spoken for. She and Moose Harmon had been sweethearts for years. Though Jordan had never witnessed a display of overt heat between the couple, she'd expected—as had the whole town—that the two would marry.

Just as the town had expected Jordan to marry Randall.

"Gatlin's was buzzing with gossip," he said. "Shoot-outs at weddings, Brockner being shoved into early retirement and taking off in a snit to dork around with his flowers, the school principal getting railroaded into the position of sheriff.'' Twin dimples appeared in his cheeks. ''The general consensus is a feisty photographer should have been the one to run for the job. Seems she's got a dead-eye aim with film canisters.''

Jordan grinned. ''That'd be Charity Arden.''

''Ah, Bud Arden's sister. Local kids still sneaking out to their farm to get the pigs drunk?''

''Yes.'' She controlled a giggle. ''And I think that's just awful!''

''Yeah, well, we've got more awful things to worry about right now. Like keeping you out of the hands of some seriously determined kidnappers.''

The statement snatched away her mirth. ''You don't think they'll give up?''

''Not according to what I heard last night…and saw today.'' He pulled the ransom note out of his pocket, rubbing the paper between his blunt fingers. ''Makes you wonder about Grazer's Corners. Bunch of nuts infiltrating. And I don't mean the almond trees.''

Chapter Five

Tanner saw her eyes grow worried again, and regretted that he'd thrown the stark reminder at her. Even with the heels snapped off her shoes, she was still a fairly tall woman. The smooth definition of feminine muscles in her arms told him she was used to physical work. By her own admission, she preferred to do things herself, rather than rely on others.

So why was he feeling so protective? Human nature, he told himself. Aside from the emotions he had tied up in Jordan Grazer, it was in his blood to protect. He'd do it for anyone.

"I should call home," she said.

"I'd rather you didn't."

"But Daddy will be worried sick."

Once again, her concern was for someone other than her fiancé. He filed that information away, decided not to bring it to her attention. "I'd rather he worry and you be safe, instead of turning that worry into something real and dangerous. We're a step ahead if we're just looking for kidnappers. If we had to add you to the official Missing list, the stakes would be more dicey."

"You and I know that, but Mother and Daddy don't."

He tried to put himself in her shoes, couldn't quite stretch his imagination that far. He'd never had anyone who gave a damn whether or not he came home—other than Mr. B. But he wasn't a blood relation.

Surprising himself, he went against every instinct he possessed. "If you want to call, I won't stop you. I'm still advising against it, though."

"I have to. I can't put my parents through this. Daddy's still distraught over what happened to Kate Bingham—and she's not his daughter."

"I didn't realize there was a connection between Maynard and Katie."

"Daddy's head of the school board. Since Kate's parents are gone, she asked him to walk her down the aisle at her wedding."

"The botched wedding," he reminded her. "Interesting that two weekends in a row disaster struck at events where Maynard held center stage." He felt a niggling of distrust. Probably just his own emotions cluttering up his mind.

When Jordan drew in a sharp breath, Tanner was sorry he'd voiced the thought.

"Are you suggesting my father had something to do with all this?" Her tone was indignant, hurt.

He felt like a heel. "Sorry, that was uncalled-for. I was just talking off the top of my head, grabbing at straws."

"You definitely came up with the short one."

Her steady gaze made him feel hot under the collar—and in other places.

"Look, Jordan, there's no law in Grazer's Corners

at the moment. I'm your best bet for safety, and I have an annoying habit of liking things done my way."

"Then I imagine we're going to butt heads. I'm fairly big on control myself."

"That so? Seems to me a woman in control wouldn't be marrying some guy she doesn't want to."

"I never said I didn't want to marry Randall."

"Didn't have to. It's pitifully obvious you don't even have the hots for the guy."

She fairly bristled with indignation. "I don't see how you can say such a thing."

"I just did." He barely controlled the smile that tugged at his lips. He folded his arms, leaned against the counter, prepared to enjoy the show.

She didn't disappoint him.

"What's this?" She hooked her hands at her waist. "Mr. Easy Rider's into psychoanalyzing?"

"Doesn't take a shrink to read you, duchess." He winked at her, enjoying the icy fire that lit her green eyes. "I might not have all the details yet, but I'll figure it out."

"Like hell," she muttered.

"I always did enjoy a challenge," he mused aloud. "If you're set on making that call, I'll get the cell phone out of my duffel."

"This one's not hooked up?" Distracted, she glanced at the portable resting on the countertop.

"Nope. Dead as ashes. Even if it was, the line's traceable. Granted, those two goons didn't look like they could find their way out of a paper bag, but I've never been one to underestimate my opponent. Appearances are often deceiving." Like Jordan

Grazer's. He'd been half prepared for an uppity debutante. But she was as down-to-earth as the next woman, only falling back on snootiness as a smoke screen when she felt threatened.

He was damned well looking forward to shaking up that peaceful world of hers a little more. He wasn't usually wrong about people. And if Jordan Grazer was in love with uptown Randall Latrobe, Tanner would eat his favorite leather jacket.

Though her present situation wasn't a joking matter, Tanner suddenly felt buoyant. The race wasn't in the bag just yet with regard to Jordan's affections.

"Marrying someone you didn't love," he muttered in disgust as he went to retrieve the mobile phone. If ever a woman needed saving from herself, it was Jordan.

And Tanner figured he just might be the man to do it.

If he got a broken heart in the bargain, what the hell. It wouldn't be the first time he'd stepped off the deep end and fallen flat on his face.

With the tiny phone cupped in his hand, he went back into the house. Security was his business, so he'd made sure this little honey couldn't be breached by the Pentagon itself.

He saw her jerk when he closed the door. For all her bravado, she was a bundle of nerves. He didn't blame her.

"Easy," he said softly. "Just me."

She didn't hold his gaze. Beneath her nerves was fire. And that wasn't masculine pride talking. He knew it because he felt it himself.

Before he could get any more sidetracked, he

flipped open the phone, punched in a series of numbers to scramble the signal, then handed it to her.

"Make it brief, Blackie."

"What should I say?"

"Just tell him you're fine. Don't mention me or where we are."

"What if he gets a ransom note? The kidnappers could still send one. I don't want Daddy putting out money when I'm perfectly fine."

This phone call was about to open a can of worms Tanner didn't want to set loose. "I changed my mind." He took the phone back from her. "We'll hold off for a bit."

She made a grab for the instrument. "But I need to give him instructions for my horses." As an obvious afterthought, she added in a rush, "I have to make sure he tells Randall not to worry. I need to—"

He touched a finger to her lips, watching as her eyes went wide, then darkened to emerald. He knew where her priorities lay. With her animals. And that was what he would concentrate on. To hell with the wimpy fiancé.

"Let me get the ball rolling on the investigation. I've got someone in mind who can care for your stables until we get back."

"Who?" she demanded. "I don't trust strangers around my horses. Bleu's a sweetheart, but he can be ornery, especially if he doesn't know you."

"Sonny's a good man. He'll have that stallion eating out of his hand within minutes."

"I don't know," she said, worry knitting her brow. "It makes me nervous. One look at Honor Bleu and you know he's Kentucky Derby stock. He loves to run. It's in his blood. But if you handle him wrong—''

"Blackie?"

"What?"

"Trust me."

She closed her eyes, let out a weary breath. "Do I have a choice?"

"Everybody has a choice. At the moment, I'm trying to make sure yours isn't taken from you."

She nodded. "Go ahead and make the call. I've got a killer headache, and the thought of being bound and gagged and stuffed in somebody's trunk doesn't appeal." She started to turn away, then stopped. "Tanner?"

"Hmm?"

"Thank you for rescuing me. Contrary to what you might think, I'm really not spoiled and ungrateful."

It took everything he possessed not to reach for her, to soothe, to press her against his heart and hold on. "I know that, baby," he said, emotion tightening his throat.

He turned his back and punched in Samuel Bartholomew's number. If he kept looking at Jordan, he'd do something he'd be sorry for. He'd push. God knew, he was no gentleman. But still..."

The line engaged.

"Samuel, here."

"Mr. B.," Tanner said, feeling steadier just hearing his friend's voice.

"Tanner, my boy," the man boomed. "How's the lake?"

"Serene as ever. I've run into a little snag, though, and could use your help." He told his friend

about Jordan and the kidnapping attempt. ''I doubt
that anyone will find us out here, but it's not feasible
for me to go snooping around town.''

''I see your problem. Especially since the good
folks in town saw you whisking the bride away.''
Mr. B. chuckled. ''How can I help?''

''I thought maybe you could send Sonny to poke
around.''

''Ah, an investigation. I'd be tickled to spearhead
it for you. Always did fancy myself a bit of a
sleuth.''

''Now don't go getting carried away.'' He had
visions of Jessica in ''Murder She Wrote,'' under-
going a gender change. Mr. B. delighted in sticking
his fingers in every pie around. And like Midas, everything he touched turned to gold.

But this particular moneymaking scheme wasn't
to their benefit. The pockets waiting to be padded
belonged to a couple of yokels he'd yet to put a
name to.

But he would.

''Just give me a sketchy outline of your plan, son,
and I'll run with it.''

''I'd thought to have Sonny run with it,'' Tanner
said, grinning to himself. He could just picture Samuel Bartholomew, sitting in his burgundy leather
chair, tipped back, puffing on a cigar. He heard the
creak of springs, knew the exact minute his friend's
feet came off the polished mahogany desk and hit
the floor.

''I'm no spring chicken, but I've got a few miles
left in this old body,'' Samuel reminded. ''Wouldn't
take nothing for me to zip down there and have a

look-see. The Rolls is due for a road trip—blow the cobwebs off her.''

Tanner chuckled. ''In Grazer's Corners? A Rolls will stand out like a bull in a dish shop.''

''Oh. Good point. I'll buy an American-made economy job. That new little Mustang with the 5.0 under the hood's a sweet machine.''

That was the thing about money. If one of your possessions wouldn't do, just pick up another. Tanner was in a position to make frivolous purchases like that himself. But years of living in poverty made his instincts lean toward the frugal.

''A 5.0's not exactly economy. If you've got a yen, though, go ahead and buy it—provided it's a convertible,'' he added. He appreciated a cool car as much as the next man. ''But stay close to home with it. I need a contact point, Mr. B.''

''Yes, of course. You'd know best.'' A tinge of disappointment colored his voice. ''How shall I direct Sonny?''

''Send him to Grazer's Corners to hang around, see if anyone's talking. I figure the best place for a home base would be Maynard Grazer's place.''

''The girl's family?''

''Yeah. If the perps are watching for her, that's where they'll look. And it'll serve two purposes.'' He explained about Jordan's horses, her worry. ''I need somebody in there that I can trust. Sonny's the best man I know.''

''Definitely qualified. He's done an excellent job with my stables, and I'm probably more persnickety about my animals than your Jordan is.''

''Neck and neck.'' With Jordan edging into the lead.

"Hmm. Sounds like a lady I'd like to meet."

"She's a little young," Tanner said, the smile in his voice holding no censure.

"Mr. B. laughed. "Young or old. No matter. You know how I love women."

Tanner grinned, not bothering to call the man's bluff. Samuel Bartholomew was a handsome, eccentric millionaire. He loved a good adventure, romance novels and a well-told joke. As for his teasing statement about women, Mr. B.'s one true love had died thirty years ago, before they'd even had a chance to marry. And in all those years, there'd never been anyone to replace Samuel's Ellie.

"I'll leave the cell phone on. Keep me posted."

He ended the call, turned and nearly bumped into Jordan.

Her eyes held a spark of defiance.

"Don't say it, Tanner. It's not eavesdropping when it involves my life."

"And your horses."

"Well?" she prompted.

With Jordan around, Tanner couldn't keep his mind on business as usual. He had a hard time holding a train of thought. Damn, she smelled good. Something sweet, delicate, springtime fresh. He pulled his thoughts back to her question. "Sonny should be there first thing in the morning."

"Can I call home now?"

He cleared the code, punched in another and handed her the phone. "Keep it short and vague."

"Should I tell him to expect your man? Daddy's funny about outsiders. He won't let somebody just take up residence."

"You've got a bunkhouse in the barn, don't you?"

"Yes."

"Then Sonny will talk his way into it."

"I hope you're right," she said and dialed the phone.

Tanner stayed close, just in case she got too chatty and he was forced to end the call.

"Daddy? It's Jordan.... I'm fine.... No, really, just listen. I'm safe.... I'm with—"

Tanner touched her shoulder, shook his head.

"I'm with a friend. If you get a demand for money, disregard it. It's a hoax.... I *can't* come home just now. Don't worry about me. Take care of my horses, Daddy, and tell Mother—" her gaze darted to Tanner's "—and Randall that I'm fine."

She paused, and Tanner held out his hand, signaling it was time to end the call.

"I'm sorry about the wedding and the money," she said in a rush. "I love you, Daddy. I'll call again soon, but I've got to go now. Don't worry."

She closed her eyes, feeling the press of tears, and handed him the phone.

"You did good, Blackie."

"He had so many questions. I felt awful not answering them."

"At least he knows you're safe."

THE WORST OF HER headache had subsided, but she still felt out of sorts, ungrounded. Tanner had gone out to put the motorcycle in the garage—hiding the getaway vehicle, she guessed.

Sitting on the end of the dock, she glanced at the sleek powerboat bobbing gently in the wooden boat slip. She wondered who used the sporty pleasure craft, and why it had been left in the water. Had Tanner been here for a while?

She found it odd that he'd suddenly turn up in town—the day before her wedding.

So many questions, she thought. Up until today, her life had been fairly normal. Now it had turned into some crazy adventure...with a handsome hero in the starring role.

Unwilling to dwell on that scenario, she glanced at her surroundings. It was hard to believe they were actually so close to Grazer's Corners. This place seemed another world away. So serene.

Sprawling acres of grass and oaks surrounded the freshwater lake. Automatically, she pictured where horse stables should be. And a barn, she decided, to the west, with pristine whitewashed fences to enclose an exercise pen.

The handicapped kids would love it here. The place begged for the sound of children, voices raised in excitement as they frolicked with the animals or splashed in the cool water of the lake.

Little Annie would love the boat, would be thrilled to ride with the wind whipping her wiry pigtails.

Feeling silly for getting swept away with the vision, Jordan inhaled, letting the clean, loamy smell of earth and lake water clear the last of her headache.

She heard the weatherworn boards of the dock creak, felt the heat of Tanner's body as he eased down beside her. He'd taken his hair out of the ponytail she'd fashioned. With a slight curl, it hung thick past his shoulders. She nearly reached out to touch, but controlled the impulse, sparing a thought for the bridegroom she'd left behind—though not deliberately.

Randall wouldn't appreciate her thoughts or her impulses toward another man.

"Your eyes aren't looking quite so pinched," Tanner commented. "Headache gone?"

"Pretty much. The fresh air's helped." Not to mention Tanner's massage. "This is a really restful place. I can see why your Mr. B. would choose it."

"He bought the place years ago. For the woman he was in love with."

"What happened?"

"She died before they could marry."

"Oh, that's sad." Their shoulders bumped as he sent a rock skipping over the water's surface.

"It was a long time before he could bear to come here, before he decided to build."

"He built this place for her? Even after she was gone?"

"He built it for love. His Ellie loved water and horses and wide-open spaces."

"A man who believes in romance," she said softly.

"Russell's not the romantic type?"

"Randall," she corrected, suspecting he kept getting the name wrong on purpose. "And we were discussing your friend. Which is funny, actually, because I was just thinking this land fairly begged for horses and stables."

"That was the intention. I think it's still too painful for him to spend a lot of time here. He keeps the stables in Fresno."

"Sounds like he's pretty well-off to have several residences."

"The man's got money to burn."

"So how did you meet him?"

He glanced at her, his eyes unreadable. "You mean, what's poor white trash like me doing with a moneybags like Mr. B.?"

Jordan ground her teeth, which made her aware that the dull ache was still lurking at her temples after all. "It's taking all of my good breeding not to push you off this dock for a statement like that."

His mouth kicked up in a slight grin. "Old habits are hard to break."

"Make the effort," she advised. "I've never once considered you poor white trash."

"So you've considered me?"

There was a trap here. Jordan was sure of it. Especially when she noticed the spark of amusement in his whiskey eyes. She walked into it anyway. "Now and again."

"That's something, since we never moved in the same circles."

She sent him another warning look.

"That's not a put-down, duchess. It's fact."

"Well, here's another fact, ace. We're out in the middle of nowhere, with a couple of throwbacks from the sixties very likely lurking in the shadows and bent on my abduction. There are no invitations to cotillions sitting on the hall table, no country-club couples to watch our every move." She shoved a flyaway strand of hair off her face. "Nor are there any migrant farmworkers hunkered around a fire."

She was almost sorry she'd made that last reference; she saw the way his jaw tightened.

His father had been one of those farmworkers—drunk more often than sober.

But she was too irritated by his attitude to quit now. "There's just you and me, Tanner. And like it or not, opposite backgrounds or not, we need to get along."

"Fierce little thing, aren't you? You always were a champion of the underdog."

"Are you lumping *yourself* in that category?" The idea was so absurd she surprised herself by laughing out loud. "Nobody looking at you would ever accuse you of being an underdog."

His smile edged up, mirroring hers. "At least not to my face."

"Tough guy," she muttered, looking around, unable to hold his gaze. When he smiled, she wanted to melt. "Who do the cows belong to?" A Holstein and her calf stood in a clump of knee-deep grass that grew between centuries-old oaks. They lifted their black-and-white faces as though they scented the humans.

"Beats me. I've noticed them wandering around before. Must be a break in the fence somewhere."

"If they hang around we might have to put them to use. At least we won't run out of milk."

"I can't quite picture you milking a cow." Tanner picked up her hand. Creamy skin, short nails. A closer inspection revealed she was no stranger to work. Definitely at odds with that fancy face.

And she wasn't wearing an engagement ring. Curious.

"I've never actually done it before," she admitted. "I understand the concept, and I could probably do it in a pinch."

He noticed that her hand trembled slightly just before she pulled it away.

"I imagine you could do a lot of things in a pinch." It took guts to stand up against kidnappers, to ride off with a man she hadn't seen in ten years, whom she hadn't really known even back then.

Tanner kept forgetting they were near-strangers. She'd always occupied such a large portion of his thoughts and dreams, that he felt as though they were intimately acquainted.

And linking himself with Jordan intimately, even in his thoughts, was going to get him in deep trouble.

He'd learned to set goals, reasonable goals. And he'd exceeded them. But he knew not to reach for something that was unreachable, knew which field was open and which was forbidden.

Jordan was forbidden.

She belonged to another man. And to a town and family who would never accept him—no matter how much money he had.

"We're not exactly cut off from civilization," he said. "Grazer's Corners is off-limits for a while, but there's a town not far from here, up toward Yosemite. I won't make you milk the cow. We can make a run for store-bought milk and supplies if need be."

Jordan turned toward him, touched his arm. "I realize you're helping me, Tanner. I didn't mean to give the impression that I felt like a prisoner."

He shrugged, tamping down the image that sprang to mind. If he thought it would work, he'd hold her as his prisoner. For life. But he wasn't a man who liked to win by default.

"You're a good sport, Blackie. Until we hear from Sonny, I'd like to keep a low profile."

"As long as I don't have to stay cooped up in the house."

"Not in it. Just close to it…and to me."

Jordan nearly strangled on a soft breath. The way he'd said those words, like a sensual threat, had her heart pounding like a runaway Thoroughbred's.

Her gaze locked on to his and she found it next to impossible to look away. His long hair, the color of rich coffee, framed striking, masculine features, that could easily grace a movie screen. His lips looked firm and yet soft—so enticing. She felt herself sway, drawn toward him; felt dizzy and restless and wanting.

"Baby, you keep looking at me like that and I'm gonna forget this was your wedding day…along with my manners."

His words hit her like a splash of icy water to the face, jerking her to her senses.

Dear Lord, she hadn't truly realized the ramifications of their situation, hadn't fully considered the tough part….

Living under the same roof with bad-boy Tanner Caldwell.

Chapter Six

He hadn't been able to sleep. Especially knowing that Jordan was just down the hall, within touching distance. Those moss-green eyes and all that black hair... Damn. She'd haunted him for ten years. But he'd been busy, and far enough away that he'd worked past the yearning. Or had tried to.

Now, his store of control was crumbling. Being close enough to smell her, to touch, to taste... Hell, he was a basket case—and he'd spent less than twenty-four hours in her company.

If lack of sleep wasn't enough to put him out of sorts, a trip to the bathroom did the trick.

Silk stockings slapped him in the face as he reached in to twist the knobs of the shower.

Every nerve, cell, and muscle in his body came startlingly awake. Draped next to the hosiery was a pair of minuscule, white G-string panties. Hell on fire, he swore to himself, Latrobe didn't know what he'd missed on his wedding night.

And right that minute, Tanner wished he didn't know, either. He ran a hand over his face, tried to rein in his imagination.

The sexy undies made it impossible.

Swearing, he gathered the delicate feminine lingerie, laid it on the sink, then reached in and twisted the tap.

Just the one. The one marked Cold.

Nothing short of ice water would do.

A WHILE LATER, he realized he shouldn't have bothered. The smell of French roast wafted from the kitchen. The double doors stood open, and Jordan was outside, apparently gathering the last of the season's wildflowers.

He leaned against the doorjamb and watched her, tension humming through his body. She'd obviously gone through the dresser drawers where he kept extra clothes, and had appropriated one of his tank tops and a pair of sweats he'd cut off into shorts.

As she bent over, he couldn't help but notice the absence of panty lines. Since he'd *seen* that particular article of pure sin draped next to the stockings in the bathroom, it had teased his imagination, and now fueled his knowledge that she wasn't wearing underwear beneath the shorts.

He groaned. The woman, and her lack of undergarments, was going to drive him crazy.

He cleared his throat. "You're up early." He'd thought debutantes liked to sleep until noon. He wished like hell that this one would live up to a few stereotypes.

She whirled around, pressed a hand to her breasts.

Her unbound breasts.

Damn it, he was going to have to find a mall and get this woman some decent clothes. Quick. Otherwise he'd go mad...or pounce.

"You scared me," she said, clutching a fistful of cut flowers and a pair of scissors.

"Sorry."

Her chest rose as she took a steadying breath. "I'm used to being up with the horses. Even on the days Daddy wants me at the office in town, the animals still need care."

"Busy girl."

"I don't mind." She brushed by him, opening the cabinets in search of a vase. "I like having something to do." She glanced at him and smiled. "You might be sorry you stuck your neck out for me. Inactivity tends to make me cranky."

He barely refrained from suggesting an activity— a sexual one. As it was, she was like a skittish horse, flitting around the kitchen, filling a vase with water and arranging her flowers just so.

He had to admit she made the straggly blossoms look fancy. Then again, flower arranging was probably a required course among her set.

The rich smell of coffee teased his senses. He was in dire need of caffeine—and balance. Despite himself, his gaze kept straying to her shorts. "I could use a little less activity if you don't mind. Why don't you sit. You're making me dizzy."

She paused, and glanced at him. "You've beat me to the punch."

He frowned, eyeing the coffeepot. In order to get it, he'd have to come close to Jordan. He didn't trust himself not to touch. "How's that?"

"*You're* the one who's cranky." As though she'd read his thoughts, she poured a cup of coffee. "Sugar?"

"Just black."

"Sure?" she asked, her green eyes sparkling with mischief. "Your disposition could stand a dose of sweetness. Several tablespoons full, if you ask me."

"Just black," he repeated. "Are you always so chipper in the mornings?"

"Disgustingly so, according to friends and family. It's a curse."

He shook his head, raked his hair back off his forehead, and accepted the mug she held out. Already, a smile was bathing his insides. He liked that she was making the best of a strange situation. A lot of women would be wringing their hands and whining over the forced isolation.

But Jordan Grazer had grit. "Actually, your cheerfulness is kind of nice."

"See there? We're making progress."

"I didn't know we'd lost ground."

"I mean, we're cohabiting nicely."

"Depends on your definition of 'nicely.' I'm not used to fighting my way through feminine undergarments to get to the shower."

Color bloomed on her cheeks, yet she held his gaze with a saucy look. He'd seen that look before. At the bar. A challenge.

If she knew how close he was to acting on that challenge, she'd probably tear off at a run.

Then again, maybe not. More than one rich girl looking for thrills had been intrigued by him. There was something about a guy like him that drew women—the wrong kind of women.

He wondered if Jordan was aware that several of her uptown girlfriends had wanted to give him a try. It had disgusted him, really, their attitudes. They might be willing to dally with him on the sly, but they'd never think of bringing him home.

He saw the way she pinched the hem of the gray shorts, working the material between restless fingers. He realized her sassiness was a bluff. Beneath the bravado was an innate sweetness she'd never been able to hide.

Still, the contrast was enough to make him want to head back to the cold shower.

Instead, he took a sip of steaming coffee.

"Have you called your man yet?" she asked.

"I've barely got my eyes open." He noticed that she was mangling another of the dish towels. An indication of both unease and the fact that she liked to keep her hands busy.

"We can't just sit back and do nothing."

"It might seem like nothing to you, but the work's being done behind the scenes."

"That makes me nervous. I'd rather be doing something *myself*."

"You ever investigated a kidnapping attempt before?"

"No. Have you?"

"Yes."

That stopped her. "You said you're in security. What do you do, guard the President or something?"

"Close. I safeguarded Mr. B."

"Were people making attempts on his life?"

"You'd be surprised what people will do for money."

"I guess I'm coming to understand that a little more. I don't like it, though."

"Not many would. If you ask me, the world's

going to hell in a handbasket. Too many people are either eager to sue or intent on stealing. They're unwilling to work for what they want.''

"That's an awfully broad generalization. Not everyone has bad intentions. And in some cases, there are legitimate reasons to bring suit against somebody.''

"You live a sheltered life, duchess.''

"I resent that.'' She fussed with her blossoms, then went back to twisting the dish towel. "Just because I'm willing to give people the benefit of the doubt doesn't mean I'm naive. What's made you so cynical?''

"Guess I've seen the seedier side of human nature.'' He hooked an ankle around one leg of the chair, then straddled the seat, his forearms resting on the wooden back. It was a self-preservation move. In her righteous defense of mankind, her chest had expanded, clearly showing the outline of firm breasts against the skimpy cotton of the tank top. Her jet-black hair was caught up in a bouncy ponytail, making her look younger than her twenty-seven years.

"But you've seen some good, too, haven't you?''

"Some.''

"Well, then. There you have it.''

His brows grew together. "Have what?''

"An argument to counterbalance all that cynicism.''

"You're one of those who looks at the glass half-full.''

"It's a good attitude to take. Makes for a much happier disposition.''

He snorted. "I never quite learned that knack. Especially since my glass was always damn near empty."

"But you've made changes in your life," she argued.

"So?"

"So, you fill up your *own* glass, Tanner. You don't look for somebody else to do it for you."

"Ah, and here we've come full circle. In a roundabout way, you're accusing me of being just like the suers and takers." If she knew just how full his glass was—how far he'd come in life—they wouldn't be having this conversation.

Her breath hissed out in obvious exasperation. Tanner felt a grin tugging. She was not the typical uppity debutante, as he'd first thought. But she was way too trusting, in his opinion.

"You've twisted my words and missed my point," she said. "I wasn't speaking monetarily. If you'd give yourself half a chance, spend a little more time thinking positively, maybe that chip on your shoulder wouldn't be giving the Sierra Nevada a run for their money."

"Who says I've got a chip on my shoulder?" He didn't like being psychoanalyzed. Especially when the diagnosis was so accurate.

"It's plain as day. And I'm very aware that my family helped put it there."

He stood, sending the chair scraping across the tile floor. Striding to the sink, he dumped his lukewarm coffee and poured a fresh cup. He noticed that Jordan backed up a step, knew that his expression resembled a storm cloud ready to unleash a torrent of fury.

Taking a deep breath, he tried to ease the roil of

emotions. He might have a healthy bank account, but money didn't buy away loneliness, didn't erase bad memories.

"If we're going to take responsibility, let's put it where it belongs. My father was a drunk. He deserved to get fired."

She reached out to him, touched his arm. "But you didn't deserve to be abandoned."

Her eyes were soft with compassion. He didn't want her pity. And he didn't want to open those old wounds again—a shame he'd spent ten years trying to outrun.

"I was of age, Blackie. Can't really call that abandonment." But it had felt like it. He'd come home, covered with soot from fighting the fire in the Grazers' vineyards, to find the shabby travel trailer gone. Douglas Caldwell had hitched the silver bullet to the back of the pickup and skipped town, never even bothering to leave his son a farewell note.

The next day, Maynard Grazer had told Tanner that no Caldwell was ever again allowed to set foot on Grazer property. Jobless and homeless, Tanner had been forced to grow up in a hurry.

And if he really thought about it, he owed Maynard Grazer a debt of gratitude. The unfairness, and the shame, had fueled Tanner's determination to make something of himself.

Which he'd done beyond his wildest dreams.

Jordan's fingers curled around his forearm, squeezing in compassion.

"I won't apologize for having advantages, Tanner. But I want you to know that I never thought less of you...because of your family's financial status." She closed her eyes, took a breath. "That probably didn't come out right. I—I've always liked you.''

Her stammering words made his heart feel like a marshmallow. No wonder he'd never been able to get her out of his mind. She was unique.

And she was so close, her hand warm against his arm. *Just once,* he thought. Dear God, what could it hurt? He'd fantasized about her lips, her taste, for so many years. And after he was assured she was no longer in danger, he'd have to let her go.

She was promised to another man.

He might never get the chance again.

He turned, took the dish towel from her hand, noticed that her eyes had deepened to the color of rich moss.

Jordan licked her lips, unable to look away from Tanner's penetrating gaze. An undeniable current— potent and electric—charged the air in the room. She didn't know how it had happened. One minute she was offering comfort and honesty; the next, all she could think about was awareness.

Awareness of Tanner. So strong, so close, so virile. Her heart slammed against her chest as his hand slipped around her waist, drawing her closer. His long hair slid across his shoulders as he bent his head.

''I have to kiss you, Blackie,'' he whispered, his voice deep and raw with emotion. ''Stop me.''

''I can't.'' And it was the absolute truth. She couldn't have moved if her life had depended on it.

As though he feared she'd disappear, he brought his fingertips to her cheeks. So softly, so reverently, he stroked her. His eyes closed, as though he were in pain. He started to pull back. She reached up and caught his hands in hers.

"Please," she whispered. Unable to think beyond the moment, she leaned into him. As his hands cupped her face, his lips feathered against hers, nibbling, testing, savoring. She'd never known a touch could be so gentle, so full of longing.

A longing she felt, too, with every fiber of her being. Like a storm raging inside her, desperation built. She wanted the world to go away, wanted there to be no obligations or responsibilities.

She wanted to be free to explore, to accept this tenderness, to see where it would lead. She wanted to dream. About Tanner.

But she wasn't free. Through the haze of desire, that realization finally penetrated.

Reluctantly, sensibly, she pulled back.

"We have to stop." She was engaged to another man. Somewhere out there, criminals could be searching for her. She had obligations to uphold that didn't include Tanner Caldwell, obligations that would have devastating consequences for her family if she turned her back on them, if she took something for herself, took what she wanted.

And right now, she wanted Tanner Caldwell. Wanted him with a fierceness that threatened to block out reason.

She saw a muscle tick in his jaw, saw the questions in his brown eyes, the desire. Then he nodded once and let her go.

Which was a good thing. Jordan didn't think she had the strength to sever the contact on her own.

TANNER LEFT THE ROOM before he was tempted to push. Jordan's words were at odds with the message in her eyes. It was the circumstances, he told himself. He'd saved her from a kidnapping attempt. She'd naturally be grateful.

In his line of work, he'd seen how easily gratitude got confused with intimacy during a crisis, and he'd taken great care not to encourage it, to distance himself.

The problem was, with Jordan, he didn't care. He was willing to take any crumb she might offer.

And that bothered the hell out of him.

Snatching his cell phone from his duffel by the bedside, he punched in the security code and paged Sonny.

Then he sat on the side of the mattress. With elbows propped on his knees, he rested his head in his hands, his hair falling forward across his forearms.

He ought to tie the damn mass back. Keeping his hair long was an act of rebellion. He hadn't really thought about that in a while. He'd told himself it was eccentricity. Like Mr. B., people with gobs of money could do or act or dress any way they pleased.

The hair thing was more than eccentricity, though. It was his way of jutting out his chin, daring somebody to take a swing, daring somebody to judge.

Take me just like I am.

God, that cry hadn't echoed so loud in a long time.

It was because of Jordan, he realized. He wanted her acceptance, her admiration. Not because he was filthy rich. He didn't want her to see him in a different light because of his money.

He wanted her to see only *him*. The man.

The cell phone gave a low ring and Tanner jumped. Hell, where had his prided steadiness gone?

Right out the window with Jordan Grazer's powerful, coveted kiss.

Irritated with himself, his thoughts, his lack of control, he punched the Send button.

"Caldwell."

"Sonny, here. You paged?"

"Yeah. Did you get in?"

"Piece of cake. Nice spread. Gorgeous horseflesh. Grazer's a jackass, but he's worried about his little girl."

That girl wasn't so little. And if Maynard knew the thoughts Tanner had about his daughter, he'd be even more worried.

"What cover did you use?" Tanner asked.

"Told him I'd suffered a personal tragedy, didn't want wages, just board for a few weeks, a place to heal. Gave him a glowing reference from Mr. B. The horses took to me right away. Grazer was more impressed with that than with the reference."

"Good," Tanner said approvingly. Actually, the excuse wasn't too far from the truth. Sonny *had* suffered. His wife and baby had died in a fiery car accident two months ago. As for healing, it would take more than a few weeks. Sonny was hiding his pain behind work. It surprised him a little that Sonny would actually use the excuse. "You doing okay?"

"Fine." The single word was terse. Tanner knew when to back off.

"Any news?"

"I just got here."

Tanner chuckled. "I know you, buddy. What have you heard?"

"That this is a nutty town. The school principal who's also the temporary sheriff is still missing. Seems there was a town meeting last week. Moose Harmon—Kate Bingham's intended—wanted to call in the FBI. Local banker, Randall Latrobe, was adamantly against it."

Just hearing the name of Jordan's fiancé made Tanner's gut tighten. "Did he give a reason?"

"Bad publicity. Didn't want big-city media sniffing around. He's worried about the bottom line— real estate taking a dive and drying up the bank's chances for fat loans."

"Any stellar first impressions on Latrobe?"

"I'm good, Caldwell, but I'm not Superman. I stopped at the greasy spoon in town—another weird bunch in there. I met Moose Harmon and an interesting little dish he had with him—Betsy Muller. Works in his cosmetics department at the store he owns. Looks at him with moon eyes. He was looking back, which makes a man wonder, seeing as he's still engaged to the missing school lady. They were doing the talking, I was doing the listening. Being a stranger, if I'd started asking questions... Well, you know how it's done."

"Yeah."

"After that, I came straight to Grazer's. Guy's full of bluster and didn't think twice about telling a total stranger his daughter was missing. He's pretty torn up. Seems genuine, but I'll reserve judgment. I think I can talk him into confiding in me."

"It's that mug of yours. Deceiving. Invites people to spill their guts."

Sonny didn't comment. People were always telling him he was a pretty boy. Behind those blond good looks, though, was a man of steel, even lethal. Sonny was an ex-cop who'd gotten sick of the system. In much the same manner Tanner had, Sonny had hooked up with Samuel Bartholomew—by chance. Mr. B. had a knack for taking in misfits.

"Since I'm not on the payroll," Sonny said, "I'll have the freedom to come and go. I'll see to the horses, then nose around town."

"Speaking of the horses, there's a stallion who's special."

"Yeah. Honor Bleu. I've met him. He took a liking to me. Like I said, cinched my cover. I'm told he can be a mean cuss. High-hipped, black as night. Sired by Devil out of Angel. A real prizewinner."

"You be careful with that Thoroughbred," Tanner warned. "He'll need to be exercised, but leave it at that."

"Grazer mentioned something about a trauma to the leg."

"Yeah. My understanding is that it's pretty much healed. But running's in his blood. He'll give all he's got, if asked. Don't ask."

"Got it. I'll check in when I know more."

Tanner ended the call. Knowing he was stalling, he punched in a new code and checked in with his offices, both in Fresno and Modesto. It was a fairly useless call—he'd handpicked and trained his staff and they were as efficient as the Secret Service.

Both offices knew his whereabouts if needed, and Tanner was a man who knew how to delegate. Obviously, he'd done his job well. There were no glitches in the smooth-running corporations; no grievances, petty or otherwise. Outside sales had picked up three new accounts last week—standard installations, his manager assured.

Normally, Tanner would have felt pride at the efficiency, been glad for the break where he wasn't needed for consultations or tricky designs.

Instead, he felt uneasy—obsolete, almost. He'd built this company with sleepless nights, the sweat of twenty-hour days, and his own two hands. If he wasn't careful, he'd delegate himself into a life of leisure.

And that wouldn't do. It would give him too much time on his hands. Too much time to relive a certain erotic kiss, to torture himself with the knowledge that Jordan Grazer was out of his reach.

That she intended to marry another man.

Chapter Seven

Jordan wasn't used to inactivity or to being cooped up in the house. She yearned for the serenity of the outdoors, the familiar scents of her stables. Barring those, the stray heifer and her calf who kept moving in closer would have to do.

Sunlight sifted gently through the oaks, glancing off a sparkling creek. Clear water shimmered as it meandered over smooth rocks, spilling on down into the lake.

She eased onto a granite boulder and dipped her feet in the creek water, staring at the shell-pink polish on her toenails, her mind awash in chaos.

Why in the world had she let him kiss her? Invited it, even?

Oh, she'd wanted it, had ached for the touch of his hands, for that exclusive look from his ginger-colored eyes, the look that told a woman she was special, desirable, that she had his sole attention.

And what a kiss it had been! Far beyond any and all of her expectations, her fantasies. But it was wrong—wrong to yearn, to allow the intimacy that would shift their relationship, that would make living under the same roof with any sort of ease next to impossible. The shift only opened up a plethora of problems, of questions and wants and old dreams that could never be satisfied.

She'd made a vow to marry another man. Why was it so hard to remember that? Her mind immediately supplied the answer. It was because of a sexy rebel with long hair and killer dimples, a man who could exasperate her, scare her…thrill her.

A man who could kiss her like there was no tomorrow.

She felt the skin on her neck prickle, as though she were being watched. Turning, she saw Tanner.

Her heart thumped against her ribs, but she told herself to be cool, to act as though nothing had happened, as though she hadn't engaged in a kiss that had rocked her tidy little world.

He was the quintessential bad boy, looking both tough and aloof. A slight frown marred his brow. Strong arms were folded across a chest that begged a woman to explore it. Jeans, worn white in places she should *not* be looking, hugged his coiled body like a supple, sinful dream. With his hair hanging loose around his shoulders, adding rather than detracting from all that masculinity, he reminded her of a warrior of old.

Agatha Flintstone would be in her glory if she caught sight of Tanner Caldwell. The seventy-something, offbeat city clerk was a fixture in Grazer's Corners. She'd yet to find a man who could live up to her high standards, who wasn't intimidated by her no-nonsense outlook on life. Actually, it was more kooky than no-nonsense, Jordan thought. Still, Agatha made no secret of her firm belief that one day her Norman conqueror would ride into town on his snorting, spirited steed to sweep her up and make her heart go pit-a-pat.

Nobody had the nerve to tell Agatha that she was dreaming, that the only place she'd find a man like that was among the shelves of her beloved Book Nook.

Had Tanner been thirty years older, or Agatha thirty years younger, her fantasy might not have seemed so far-fetched.

He fit the bill. And he certainly made *Jordan's* heart go pit-a-pat.

She dragged her gaze back to the stream before she got any more carried away.

"You shouldn't be wandering around out here." His voice was low, and held an edge that made her tremble—with renewed desire, not fear.

These reactions had to stop. *Think of Randall,* she lectured herself.

"You told me we were isolated. What's the harm?"

"The harm is, we're playing by my rules. I want you where I can see you."

"I don't remember agreeing to any rules. And you can see me now." Although that wasn't such a good thing. Especially with that kiss hanging between them. "Did you get all your calls made?"

He eased down beside her on the rock, the tips of his boots mere inches from the damp edge of the creek. She tried to scoot over and nearly fell off the sloped edge.

"Eavesdropping, Blackie?"

She rolled her eyes, figuring it wouldn't be wise to tell him she'd hoped to borrow that little cell phone when he'd left the room. But he'd taken it with him.

"I've told you before, it's not bad manners to listen if the call involves me. However, I object to skulking in hallways, so I'll just have to trust that you'll keep me abreast of what's going on." She frowned at the cows who were wandering ever closer. "Although I don't understand why *you* can have marathon conversations and *I'm* limited to two measly minutes." Not nearly enough time to put her father's mind at ease. She hated not knowing what was going on, didn't like feeling so out of control.

"It's my phone."

Though reasonable, his tone held a hint of challenge. She rarely backed down from a dare.

"You have to sleep sometimes," she taunted.

He picked up on her train of thought, and grinned. "Nobody knows the unlock code but me. You could dial away to your heart's content, duchess, and never get past the tone of push buttons."

"Smugness in a man is an unbecoming trait." A school of minnows swam with the creek's current, scattering when they came upon her pink-tipped toes. *Better the kidnapper you know...* Never had she thought she would be such a *willing* prisoner.

"Did you find out anything?"

"It's early yet. Sonny's just gotten there and settled in at the bunkhouse."

"My bunkhouse?"

"Yeah."

"That surprises me." Her knee bumped his and she swiftly drew it back. "Daddy let him?"

"I told you, Sonny's good."

"But my horses—"

"Are fine. Honor Bleu's behaving like a gentleman."

"That'll be the day. He has an ornery streak a mile wide. And he's not overly fond of men."

"Likes to be the only stud on the ranch, huh?"

She thought about the magnificent stallion, his pride, his spirit, his animalistic *maleness*. "He's very good at what he does."

"Servicing all the ladies? Lucky him."

She was a breeder, for heaven's sake. There was no call for her face to heat, for her heart to race, for her to feel edgy and embarrassed and… Lord, she wasn't sure what she was feeling. Turned-on? Images of Bleu covering a spirited mare blurred, drifted out of focus, became something entirely different.

Became the image of Tanner…naked, covering her—skin to skin, face-to-face.

He traced a finger down her cheek, making her jump.

"You've gone skittish on me. Seems strange that a woman with her heart set on being a top breeder goes all shy over discussing animal gender and mating habits."

"I didn't go all shy."

"Liar. You were thinking about two-legged animals. Maybe even thinking about me."

Was she so transparent? Determined to throw him off track—for her own sanity's sake—she said, "Stuff the ego, Caldwell. I was supposed to be married yesterday, remember?"

He plucked a flower that flourished in the moist earth by the creek's bank, touched the velvety spikes of the happy blossom to the tip of her nose, ran it along the curve of her bottom lip. "Guess I did forget. Understandable mistake. Especially with the taste of you still fresh on my lips."

She drew back from the feathery stroke of the flower. "I don't want to talk about that."

"The kiss? You're not going to tell me you didn't enjoy it."

No, she wasn't going to tell him that, but neither was she going to spill the truth. So she simply ignored him, hoped he'd drop the subject.

She felt him lift her hand, and jerked.

"Easy."

He closed her fingers around the stem of the buttery yellow flower that resembled a starburst. Memory, like a first rose pressed between the pages of a high-school yearbook, washed over her.

Once—at a time he probably didn't remember, a time that probably held no significance for him— he'd given her a daisy. She'd seen him walking off campus, alone...it seemed he'd always been so alone. So she'd approached him, her young girl's heart pumping with both giddiness and terror. Tanner had always thrilled her—and scared her. She hadn't known what she intended to say, she'd only known that he seemed to need someone, company, a friend. And she'd wanted to be that friend.

But he'd sneered at her. "Better run, Blackie. Bad guys like me eat little rich girls like you for breakfast...unless that's what you're after. In that case, I might be able to spare a few minutes."

She'd been so stunned, so tongue-tied, so crushed. Always strong, able to take most anything on the chin, she'd been horrified to feel the tears well.

And even more horrified that he'd seen it.

The change in him had been lightning swift. Gentleness had resculpted his handsome features; regret had shown in his eyes, and in his soft touch. "I'm a first-class ass, Jordan. You didn't deserve that." He'd sealed the apology by plucking a daisy, handing it to her.

She'd cherished that bedraggled, wilted flower as though it were gold, preserving it—not in a yearbook, but in her locked diary, a journal that held her deepest secrets, her most bittersweet yearnings.

That special flower was still in her room, at home, hoarded like a prize.

Reining in her thoughts from the past, Jordan turned her head, catching a whiff of shampoo that clung to his hair. If a person cared to delve past the mask he wore so easily, they'd see that he still had that look of a loner, of *loneliness*.

"Thank you for asking about the horses. If I'd known you were going to talk to your friend, I'd have given you some details to pass along. There's a colt I'm stabling who has special needs, and of course there's Bleu's contrariness."

"Sonny grew up on a ranch. His mother's a vet and his father's a trainer. He'll do fine by your horses."

"What did you say his last name was?"

"I didn't." He pitched a leaf into the creek. "It's Womack."

Her eyes widened. "Of the Kentucky Womacks?"

"That's them."

"My God. Their stables are legendary. They've trained more Triple Crown winners than anyone around."

"So I've heard." A dimple winked in his cheek. "Didn't I tell you to trust me?"

"It's nothing personal, Tanner. I don't trust anybody but me with the animals. I'm about to rethink that, though. What's Sonny doing in California when he could be living in that dreamy bluegrass country—on a renowned Thoroughbred ranch?"

"He's never said. Doesn't talk much about his private life."

"But as well as seeing to my horses, you believe he's qualified to look into the kidnapping attempt?"

"Yeah. He's an ex-cop."

"A bodyguard by my side and an ex-cop snooping around. Looks like I'm in good hands." Before the words were even out, her gaze fell on Tanner's hands. Strong, tanned, capable. There was a scar across one knuckle, another by the tip of his thumb. She imagined he'd spent some time making his way in life with his fists.

He never seemed totally relaxed. Although he appeared to give her his sole attention, she knew he was aware of every bird, butterfly or shift in the breeze.

The rustle of dry grass drew her attention to the mother cow and her calf who were moving ever closer. It was the darndest thing. One minute the heifer would stare, still as a doe caught in a set of high beams, and the next her big, wide face would swing to a point behind them. The action reminded her of a well-trained dog, signaling to its master that something was amiss.

And she was seriously losing it if she was drawing parallels between cows and sensitive pets.

When they lumbered forward a few more steps in

unison, she stopped twirling the flower stem between her fingers.

"What is with those cows? A few more feet and they'll be in our laps."

Tanner looked at the animals. They went still, as though scenting an opponent. An unfriendly opponent. "From the tracks around the property, I'd say they've been loose for quite a while. Evidently they've made themselves at home, and figure we're trespassers."

"They're acting awfully strange. Why do they keep looking back like that?" A rush of adrenaline shot through her. Unconsciously, she scooted closer to Tanner. "You don't suppose there's someone out there, do you?"

"Doubt it. The cows would be running scared."

His calm evaluation took some of the edge off her nerves. She felt safe with Tanner. Protected.

Protected as far as her person was concerned, she amended. Her heart was an entirely different matter.

"They're not scared of us," she countered.

"You wouldn't scare a fly."

She wasn't sure if that was a compliment or an insult. Her brow arched. "I have my moments. You, on the other hand, can definitely be terrifying. So why aren't the cows paying attention?"

He stared at her for a long, humming moment. "Maybe I'm losing my touch."

Oh, her mind wanted to find all kinds of interpretations for what he meant by "touch." "I don't think so."

"Thanks for the vote of confidence. Stay put. I'll have a look around."

"Not on your life—or mine," she amended,

jumping up from the rock when he stood. "I'll go with you."

Though he didn't actually smile, a dimple indented his cheek. "You're scaring yourself with the thought of nefarious people lurking in the bushes. Believe me, Blackie, if there was someone around, I'd know it."

His calmness made her feel foolish. She tossed her hair back, took a breath. "I doubt that you're infallible. And after yesterday, anything is possible—even probable."

"Maligning my bodyguarding abilities?" He tsked and put his hand at her back, urging her forward. "Let's go see what's spooking the Holstein."

"I didn't say they were spooked. Just acting weird." A thought struck her, making her shudder. "You don't suppose there are snakes out here, do you?"

He glanced down at her bare feet, his eyes traveling upward, lingering on her shorts—or rather, *his* shorts. She saw a muscle tick in his jaw, saw his eyes flare.

"Got a phobia, huh?"

His silky voice sent chills up her spine. Yes, she had a phobia about snakes. And she was fast developing one over the fact that she wasn't wearing underwear.

And that he knew it.

Unwilling to show a weakness, she marched ahead of him. Although she tried for dignity, it was a tough call. With a very real desire to keep her feet off the ground lest she encounter a slithery snake, she probably looked like a cocky rooster practicing a strut.

And doing a bad job of it.

Tanner caught up with her in two strides, making an effort to keep his grin under control. She lived on a ranch, spent a good deal of time outdoors. And the lady was scared silly of snakes. She also didn't like admitting to vulnerabilities.

He'd have to remember that. He knew about wearing masks. He was a master at the art. She, on the other hand, could use a few pointers. Her clear green eyes were like a sparkling window—the protection was there, but you could see right through it.

"Want a piggyback ride?"

"No, thank you," she answered primly.

He lost the battle with the grin. "Ah, the deb's back."

"Shut up, Tanner."

He chuckled, startling a robin from the tree. Evidently he'd startled Jordan, too. Her head whipped around and she stared at him as though seeing him for the first time.

He sobered. "What?"

"Nothing...I guess I'm not used to hearing you laugh."

"I might be from the wrong side of the tracks, but I'm human."

She stepped over a low sagebrush and swore when her bare heel came down on a thorny weed. "There's just the two of us here, Tanner. Isolated except for those silly cows who're following us. Cut the digs about class distinction." She hopped on one foot, brushing at her heel. "What is the matter with those animals? Shoo!"

"Be still." He knelt on one knee in front of her,

drew her onto the other, and lifted her foot. Her irritation was as plain as day. "You're going to get the thing embedded."

Her arm went around his neck for balance. "I can get it."

"Yeah, but at what price? I've got willpower, duchess, but not that much. You keep hopping around—without a stitch of underclothes on—and I swear I'm gonna get ideas."

She went utterly still. Her breasts beneath the flimsy tank top pressed into his chest. The barrier of her shorts might just as well have not been there. He could feel every contour of her compact body. Balanced on his knee, her outer thigh brushed against a part of him that was already achingly hard.

He'd been in that state since he'd first laid eyes on her at Gatlin's, dressed for sin and out for trouble.

She was causing a hell of a lot of trouble with his libido, with his control.

He extracted the sticker, and ran his thumb over her heel. Her soles were roughened, as though she was used to going barefoot.

He raised his head, his gaze slamming into hers. God Almighty, this woman was his dream. It seemed he'd been waiting for her all his life. He tightened his hands around her waist, pushing her thigh more firmly against him, torturing himself.

But he couldn't let her go, couldn't look away. He saw the nervous sweep of her tongue over those pink, pouty lips and felt as though something vital had short-circuited in his brain.

The groan that escaped his throat surprised him.

He could no more have stopped himself at that moment than he could have sprouted wings and flown.

Cupping the back of her head, he drew her to him, so close, lips barely touching.

"God, you're beautiful." He feasted, angling her head, drawing in her essence. Sweet. So sweet. The urgency that swept him raged like an unstoppable bullet. He couldn't think. Could only feel.

He couldn't remember this ever happening in his life—to have his mind blanked of everything but a woman.

Everything but Jordan Grazer.

The loss of control scared him. He wanted to lay her down on the bed of grassy earth, to peel away the flirty barrier of cotton that enticed rather than hid, to make love with her under the canopy of leaves overhead, to explore every facet of her firm body right here in the summer shade of the California oaks.

Her fingers tangled in his hair and all the strength went out of his knees. From his crouched position, he eased them to the ground, still holding her in his lap. Desire shot straight over the top as he realized that she'd taken over the kiss, was calling the shots, making him burn. The strength of her fingers in his hair, the avidness of her mouth moving across his, exploring, enticing, wiped his brain of all coherent thought.

Without permission, he jerked at the hem of her tank top, slid his hand beneath, and cupped her smooth breast. Her nipples were pebble hard, straining against his thumb. God, this woman had fire— damn near outmatched him.

The raspy low of a cow penetrated the mist of

desire, bringing him to his senses. His head shot up, alert, his instincts kicking in, searching for danger.

He felt the beat of Jordan's heart beneath his hand.

"What is it?" Her voice was breathless, aroused.

He gave himself a moment before he tried to speak. Years of living on the edge told him that danger didn't lurk. But something was disturbing those cows. He glanced down at Jordan. She seemed unaware that her hand covered his where it still rested over her breast.

He knew the instant that realization dawned. Color bloomed on her face, and she snatched her hand away, struggling to get to her feet.

"Easy does it, Blackie." He stood and helped her up, noticing that she looked everywhere but at him. He decided the cows could wait for another minute or two. "There's something between us. What just happened was inevitable. I'm not going to apologize."

She tugged at the hem of her tank top, molding the material to her breasts. He nearly lost his train of thought.

"I should be apologizing to Randall," she said, her voice breathy. "This isn't right. I can't..."

The sound of his hopes cracking rang in his ears. Always on the outside looking in. He didn't make a habit of poaching on another man's territory. Except this didn't feel like poaching.

He'd always viewed Jordan as his. He'd found her first. Loved her first.

His heart stopped for a split second, then revived with a painful thud. Where the hell had that thought come from?

Feeling frustrated, angry, confused, he whirled around, scowling at the cows, yet speaking to Jordan. "Either watch out for the sticker patches or stay put. In fact, that's the best idea. I'll take a turn around the property and make a lot better time than if you're pussyfooting over every little rock in the ground."

"Well, aren't we simply charming?" she said sarcastically. "I don't pussyfoot and I can keep up just fine. Besides, far be it from me to bend your rules."

"What rules, damn it." He didn't remember his gut ever being so twisted in knots.

"To keep me in your sight. If that sends you into flights of lust—well, deal with it." She arched a brow at one of the cows. "Don't just stand there. Let's go."

"Are you talking to me?" Tanner's scowl deepened. Her indignation set a match to his desire all over again. And he wasn't going to be bossed around. If anybody did the bossing, it would be him.

"If I were speaking to you, I'd be looking you square in the face. I was letting the bovine know I'm willing to go along with their bloodhound tendencies. Now, would you like to lead, or shall I?"

He glanced down at her bare feet. Releasing a pent-up breath, he maneuvered her behind him and hoisted her onto his back.

She yelped, struggling to get her legs wrapped around him before she ended up in a heap on the ground. He locked his arms around her knees, preventing her from slipping.

"You're not carrying me piggyback."

"Funny. Looks like I'm doing just that." He tightened his hold on her knees, letting her know she wouldn't get down unless he wanted her to. It was a petty show of control, but damn it, he was off-balance. And he didn't like it one bit.

Jordan held on to his shoulders. Short of struggling and sending them both on a headlong course with disaster, she appeared to be stuck. With desire still whipping through her body, the position made her much too aware of him. His long hair tickled her cheek and clung to the perspiration on her neck. Her breasts nestled against his back and with each stomping step he took, the friction at the juncture of her thighs nearly drove her crazy.

Dear heaven, she was a mass of runaway hormones. This was an entirely new side of herself—one she hadn't known existed. With her limited sexual experience, she viewed the act as so-so. She'd never understood what all the fuss was about.

Now, with only a few kisses—hot kisses, she amended—she was fast revising her opinion on the subject. This could be a very big deal. If she responded this fiercely when they'd only gotten to second base, Lord help her if they went all the way.

Which was out of the question. *Get a grip, Jordan.*

She was *not* going to go all the way with Tanner Caldwell. No matter how intriguing the possibility was. She'd hang out until his friend, Sonny, dug up some information. Not a second longer.

Then it was back home for her, to an interrupted marriage that needed to be set back on track, and a loan that would ease financial burdens and save her beloved stables.

Her hands tightened on his shoulders as a foreign sound intruded on her inner tirade, blending softly, pitifully, with the twitter of birds and rustle of leaves in the breeze.

"What was that?"

"Sounded like a whine."

"Over there." She let go of one shoulder to point to a pile of dry foliage heaped against the tree trunk. "Oh, Tanner, it's puppies!"

His hands slipped around to her hips to steady her as he lowered her to the ground. The friction of her body sliding against his strong back nearly derailed her thoughts.

But the sight of the mixed-breed mutt and her puppies stole her attention.

"Careful," Tanner cautioned as she reached out. "She looks pretty bad. If she's in pain she might bite."

Jordan noticed that Tanner didn't exercise the prudence he warned.

"It's okay, girl," he said softly, reaching out to the dog. She appeared to be a mix of shepherd and collie, with a few other unknowns thrown in. "You're having a rough time all by yourself, aren't you."

The gentleness of his tone made Jordan go all soft inside. Those scarred hands stroking so tenderly were at odds with the look of him—long hair shifting across his broad shoulders, his warrior's body crouched. Dragging her gaze from the tempting sight of him, she squatted by his side, lifting the two puppies that couldn't have been more than a few days old.

"Oh, they're so tiny. And weak."

The mother dog thumped her tail, keeping a nervous, watchful eye on her puppies. As though she'd decided that Jordan was friend rather than foe, she dropped her head wearily to the leaf-strewn earth, her woeful brown eyes trained on Tanner as though she recognized his strength, his capability, and was pleading for help.

Tanner ran his fingers over the dog's matted fur, checking for injuries. "The puppies are a good size. Looks like she had a tough delivery." His voice was like a whisper on the breeze, pitched to soothe, so he wouldn't startle the distraught, weak animal.

"We should get her to a vet." She inhaled the unique smell of puppy, noticing the scowl on Tanner's face as he took his eyes off the mother for a moment.

"Don't look at me that way," she said, knowing his thoughts before he even spoke. "Surely there's a town close by that's safe." She held the warm babies against her chest, their puppy breath tickling her neck. "Antoinette is counting on us."

He frowned. "Antoinette?"

"We can call her Annie for short."

"Why?"

"Because Antoinette can be a tongue twister."

"No. Why would you name this dog in the first place, and why Annie?"

"Because it's pretty. Feminine. She's had a rough time and she deserves a pretty name. I always wanted to name one of my horses Queen Anne, but I haven't owned one yet who fits."

"Any other significance here?"

"Like what?"

"You tell me."

The man was more astute than one had a right to

be. "All right. I've always wished I had a feminine name. Jordan sounds like a boy's name."

"I've got to tell you, Blackie, you don't look anything like a boy."

The way his eyes traveled over her, she didn't *feel* like one, either. Still, she'd spent her life living up to a certain image, the knowledge that she'd never be the son her father had so desperately wanted. The closest he'd been able to come was a unisex name.

"Sight unseen, though, it can create any number of problems. When I enrolled in college, they assigned me a male roommate."

That flash of a dimple winked again, but he didn't smile. "Did you keep him? The roommate."

She buried her face in the fur of the puppies. She hadn't actually *kept* the guy…just gone out with him a few times. But the territorial light in Tanner's eyes—a light that looked an awful lot like jealousy—spurred the imp in her.

"A true lady never discusses her liaisons." She should have known better than to poke at him. If his eyes got any hotter, her skimpy clothes would ignite and burn right off her body. "Are we going to find that vet, or not?"

He gave a nod and carefully scooped Annie into his arms. Jordan felt the need to help, to support, but her own hands were occupied with the wiggly offspring.

When she turned, she noticed the cows had caught up. Like nervous sentries in charge of the nation's gold, they watched the human activity.

"It appears those cows have the blood of Lassie in them. At least the mother does. Don't you think that's sweet? Being a mother herself, she was concerned over these babies.''

Tanner just snorted and looked down at her feet. ''You're on your own till we get back to the house.''

Her brow arched. He obviously wasn't interested in her interpretation of the cow's behavior—though she herself was feeling fairly proud of explaining the puzzling, uncharacteristic bovine sociability. And why had his tone turned so frigid?

''Despite your ideas to the contrary, I've been walking for quite a few years. And speaking of transportation—''

''I didn't know we were.''

''Walking,'' she reminded, noticing how carefully he cradled Annie in his arms, picking his way across the uneven ground so as not to jostle her. ''How are we going to manage three dogs and the two of us on a motorcycle?''

''Who said anything about the two of us?''

''I did.'' She saw his jaw clench, and gave him a look that warned him she was fully prepared to argue. And win.

''Mr. B. keeps a Jeep in the garage,'' he finally said.

''Oh. Isn't that handy.''

He didn't comment.

She was walking a few paces in front of him. At his silence, she glanced over her shoulder. ''You sure there's a vet close by? I could probably get Malone up here—he's the doctor I use at the ranch. He'd be discreet.''

''That won't be necessary.'' His voice sounded winded, yet he didn't appear to be struggling with Annie's weight.

"You sure?"

"Positive." Slowly, his gaze lifted from her behind. "And while we're in town, we're definitely getting you some underwear."

Chapter Eight

"Do you know where you're going?" Jordan asked as they strolled down a street that could have doubled as a backdrop for a Western. The sidewalks were wood plank, for heaven's sake.

The quaint little town was just west of Yosemite. They'd left Annie and her puppies at the local animal clinic where Dr. Eldon had shooed them out of his way, telling them he needed elbowroom to work. He'd have a better idea of the animals' health in about an hour.

In the meantime, he'd given them a list of supplies they'd need on hand if they were going to keep the dogs.

Jordan had been adamant that they would.

Tanner hadn't even batted an eye.

And for that, his tally of assets had skyrocketed in a flash. Randall would have had a fit, launched into an immediate argument. Of course, he did have his allergies to consider.

"The general store just up ahead," Tanner replied. "Where the old codger's keeping guard."

Jordan saw the frail man who was sitting in an ancient rocking chair. As they approached, the chair creaked to a halt. Watery blue eyes, drooping at the corners yet shrewd, watched them.

"Howdy folks. Stop by for a visit?"

"Just passing through," Tanner said.

"Well, come closer. Let me have a look, make sure you ain't one of them suckers on the Most Wanted list what hangs in the post-office window."

"You have Wanted posters in your post office?" Jordan asked, intrigued.

"Yep. And I aim to collect me a reward one of these days. Nobody's gonna beat old Hiram Birkenshire out of that money."

Dutifully, Tanner and Jordan moved closer. The old man frowned, then nodded—somewhat sadly, it appeared.

"Don't look criminal-like. I'll give you a good piece of advice, though. Stay clear of them old biddies down to the veterans hall. Damn women'll call the sheriff on pretty near everybody—even their own kin."

"Why's that?" She saw Tanner stiffen and touched a hand to his arm. She knew he didn't want them drawing attention to themselves, but she doubted they had anything to fear from old Hiram.

"They figure on beatin' me to the reward money. Course, you might escape their notice today."

He paused, obviously waiting for someone to voice a curiosity. Tanner didn't look all that interested—he still appeared to be debating the wisdom of their trip to town—but Jordan was charmed by the old man. "What's so special about today?"

"Talent-show rehearsal. Fool women are all dressed up like those derelict chickens on the commercial. Telling foul jokes no decent God-fearing woman should even know about.''

He snorted, and bobbed his nearly bald head.

Jordan smothered a laugh. She noticed that Tanner's expression had eased into amusement. ''Foul?''

''Well, dirty foul or chicken fowl, take your pick. I tell you, it ain't right.'' The old man pinned Jordan with a look. ''You steer clear, missy, ya hear? A young thing like you shouldn't hear such talk.''

''Yes, sir.''

''Good. You here to shop?''

''Yes.''

''Well, go on in. Thelma'll see to your needs. Now there's a woman who's got some sense to her—though she can be a might uppity.'' Hiram looked at Tanner. ''You get tired of pokin' around in the store, come on back out here and sit a spell.''

Tanner nodded. ''I will. If not this trip, then the next.''

''That'll do. I ain't going no place.''

Tanner gripped Jordan's elbow and steered her into a general store that seemed to carry everything from pickles to toilet-bowl chains.

Instead of the baby bottles and dog food the vet had instructed them to get, Tanner went straight to the women's apparel section. When she saw the package he reached for, she had to object on principle.

''That's not the right size.''

He glanced down at her jeans, and she nearly rolled her eyes. She'd certainly had enough sense to change her clothes before coming to town—and to wear the single pair of panties she possessed.

He stuffed the package back on the shelf, and grabbed the next size.

"Give me that, for heaven's sake." She snatched the serviceable cotton briefs out of his hands. "I'm twenty-seven, not eighty-seven. And although I appreciate a cotton strip in the crotch, I prefer nylon or silk against my behind."

"Duchess, you're playing with fire here. You pick out some sexy undies and that's all I'm gonna be able to think about. Be smart and go for the all-cotton jobs. The big ones."

As though in silent battle, their gazes locked. Jordan knew better than to engage in this type of sparring, but she couldn't seem to stop herself. She kept losing sight of her dilemma—that her life had been threatened. Instead, she continually slipped into complacency, feeling as though she were on some glorious adventure.

It might be wrong, but it felt good.

"If the thought of knowing what kind of underwear I'm buying is a problem for you, wait outside."

"Somebody's got to pay for the merchandise."

"I'll pay for them...well, I'll pay you back, at least." She held out her palm. "Just give me the money and either step outside or close your eyes. You shouldn't even be in this particular department in the first place. Just look at that woman over there. She's scandalized."

His dimple winked and this time his lips curved up to match it. He never took his eyes off her. "What am I going to do with you, Blackie?"

Keep me, she wanted to say. *Take me away from obligations and shaky finances and a promise to spend my life tied to a man I don't love. Smile at me. Just like that—like I'm someone really special.*

Some of her thoughts must have shown on her face. He reached out and touched her cheek. For a minute she thought he was going to kiss her—right here in the middle of Thelma's general store with the other customers looking on.

Insides quivering, she stepped back. "We have shopping to do."

Tanner noticed that they were drawing attention. There were only two other women in the store, but the heat he imagined was sparking between him and Jordan was bound to create a lasting impression. If anyone came snooping around, giving a description of Jordan, the people here were likely to remember her.

Damn. What was it about this woman that made him forget all his training, the lessons he'd learned in life, both the hard way and through careful instruction?

He reached into his pocket and withdrew a wad of bills, not bothering to count them. Taking Jordan's hand, he placed the cash in her palm. "Buy what you need. I'll be outside with Hiram."

She looked at the money, tried to hand it back. "I can't take this."

"We need supplies. Generally that requires money."

"Is this all you've got?"

His brows shot up before he could check the expression. "I think that'll cover anything you need."

"No, I didn't mean it that way. I meant... Oh, forget it. I'll just get the basics, the least amount that we can get by on. I can work within a budget."

He beat back the frustration that nearly made him blurt out that there was plenty more where that came from. He knew she was worried that he'd just given her every cent to his name.

"Forget the budget. Just buy what you need." He turned on his heel, knowing he had to get out of here. The way she jutted out that sweet chin, telling him she could stay within a budget—almost as if she were daring him to find fault—made him want to sweep her into his arms and kiss the daylights out of her.

And that would definitely create a lasting impression in this little town. As well as a memory that *he'd* never get out of his mind.

As a precaution against her thriftiness, he loaded a basket with food supplies, both practical and impractical—everybody needed a chocolate bar now and again—and set the goods on the counter.

The woman behind the cash register lifted arthritic hands over the keys. "Will this do it for you, dearie?"

"Hold off for a few minutes," he advised. "My wife's still shopping." The minute he said the word, his stomach jolted up to somewhere near his throat. As misdirection, the word was a good idea. And, man alive, what he wouldn't give if only she *were* his wife.

But she belonged to another man. He had to keep telling himself that. Even though he didn't like it one bit.

The first thing he was going to do when they got back to the lake house, was to call Sonny.

Tanner needed action, progress...an end to this

bodyguarding stint. Otherwise, his heart wasn't going to survive.

The bells over the screen door jingled as he let himself out of the store. Hiram perked up, his rocker stopping in mid-creak.

His bald head bobbed. "Had you pegged for a smart man. Shoppin's woman's work. Course, left to their own devices, they can get carried away. Ain't that just like 'em, though. Now, my Letty— she's passed on, God rest her soul—why, she was always wantin' to go on up to the Sears for a new hat or some such frippery. 'Bout put me in the poorhouse a time or two."

Tanner leaned against the wooden post that supported the roof overhang. The way old Hiram rambled on, it was clear he was lonely. And the man probably didn't miss a thing that went on in town.

Although he didn't have much experience with women spending his money, and he doubted there was one around who could put him in the "poorhouse," as Hiram called it, Tanner nodded. "Never met one yet who didn't like to shop."

"My condolences. Your missus is a purdy little thing." Hiram winked. "My Letty was a looker, too. S'pect you're a lot like me and don't mind much about the money."

Again, Tanner felt a jolt at the reference to Jordan as his wife. "I don't mind."

"Where's that motorcycle of yours?"

Tanner straightened as though someone had jerked a chain attached to his spine. So much for keeping a low profile. And with the way Hiram liked to talk, chances were the man would pass along any tidbit of information if asked.

Even to a couple of yokels in a garish hippie van.

Yes, there'd been times he'd just driven aimlessly, usually after he'd tortured himself by coming too close to Grazer's Corners—and to Jordan. He'd passed through this town before. It had been a while, though; several years, in fact. He'd found an injured calico cat on the side of the road, had ridden through town in search of a vet.

That was how he'd known Dr. Eldon practiced here. He didn't recall seeing Hiram, though.

"Don't get many outsiders around these parts." Hiram leaned forward in his chair. Tanner had an urge to steady the frail man, but resisted. Pride was a fierce thing. "I recognized you, seen you riding through. If you don't mind my sayin' so, son, you could stand a visit to the barber shop. Not that I'm passin' judgment, you understand."

Tanner shrugged, the corners of his mouth kicking up. "The ladies like it."

Hiram cackled. "I reckon you're okay. Nothing in the world wrong with a healthy ego. My Letty never made a peep about me lookin', either. Long as I didn't handle the merchandise. She'd have gotten the twelve-gauge after me. Course, any fool can tell you're crazy about your missus."

Tanner wasn't used to being so transparent. He'd have to be more careful. Through the screen door, he saw Jordan at the counter in animated conversation with Thelma. He noticed the way her gaze strayed to the telephone on the wall.

To cover his roiling emotions, he shared a man-to-man smile with Hiram, then pulled open the screen door.

"Sweetheart? We need to get moving."

She gave him a startled look—a look that segued into both guilt and challenge when she realized he'd seen her eyeing the phone.

As though dismissing him, she went right back to chatting with Thelma. Tanner wasn't quite sure what he was feeling. He'd half expected her to turn up her nose at the simple store—it was a far cry from Nordstroms.

But Jordan kept surprising him. She seemed to fit in anywhere. He'd noticed that at Gatlin's, then out at the lake, and now here. Unlike most of her friends, she didn't put on airs.

Why was it so easy for her? What did she know about life that he hadn't yet learned? Over the years, he'd trained himself to *pretend* to fit in. Away from Grazer's Corners, no one knew the pitiful stock he'd come from. So the act came easy. Here, in this small town where the people were unpretentious, he didn't have to act.

Other than masquerading as a married man.

But that was for Jordan's safety—not as a balm to the shame of his roots.

"Other than the VFW ladies impersonating chickens, have you noticed any other strange characters around lately?" It wasn't likely that anyone would come this far looking for them, especially to a town that wasn't even a speck on the map. If he'd thought so, he never would have let Jordan come with him to find the vet. Still, he liked to cover all the bases.

Hiram's shrewd blue eyes sharpened. "You in some kind of trouble, boy?"

He wasn't sure how much to give away. "My wife and I are on our honeymoon. There were a couple of jokers at the wedding who thought it would be fun to follow us out of town. I think we gave them the slip...but, you know how it is. I'd hate to have rice in the sheets or serenaders outside my hotel at three in the morning."

"Well, danged if a man doesn't need privacy on his honeymoon. Congratulations, by the way. What's the description?"

"VW bus. Dorky yellow flowers painted on the side."

"Nope. I'd remember something like that, just like I remember that loud motorcycle you was driving a while back. Trade it in on the Jeep, did ya?"

"I've still got the bike."

"Good for you. A man's gotta keep possession of his toys. If those weddin' crashers show up, you can be sure I won't tell 'em diddly-squat. A body can act real vague and senile when he's of a mind."

Tanner's lips quirked into a grin. "I appreciate it."

"Us men gotta stick together. Thelma!" he bellowed. "You gonna jaw all afternoon? Turn that filly loose. Her man's out here waiting in the hot sun. And I could use a spot of tonic, while you're at it. That Wild Turkey'll do me just fine right about now. Bring it on out here." He cackled and slapped his knee.

Tanner braced himself. The woman behind the cash register—Thelma—didn't strike him as a "Go fetch" sort of woman. He wondered if it might be best all around if he stepped out of the line of fire.

Through the screen door, he saw Thelma shuffle out from behind the counter. Though arthritis made her movements slow, determination fairly crackled in her every step.

"Now you've done it," Tanner said. "A smart man would plead insanity right about now. I know I would."

Hiram enjoyed another cackle.

"Damn your eyes, you old fossil." The screen door screeched open. "You holler any louder an' Sheriff Trahune'll be whippin' up a dust getting over here to see about the ruckus." She slapped an ice-cold bottle in Hiram's hand. "Mind the door, darlin'," she said to Jordan, who had her arms full of grocery sacks.

Tanner reached out to get the door and took the bags from her. Her amusement had him struggling to hold back his own smile. Both Hiram and Thelma had booming voices. They didn't appear to care who heard their bickering.

"Now, Thelma," Hiram complained. "If I'd wanted Coca-Cola, I'd've asked for it. Jawin's thirsty work, ya know."

Thelma harrumphed. "You just drink that soda pop and be thankful I'm in a mood for charity. Wild Turkey, indeed." She perched her hands on her ample hips. "I'll not have you drunk as a coyote on my front stoop. Next thing, you'd be holding me accountable for you missing out on the bingo game down at the schoolhouse."

Hiram shook his head. "Ain't got no notion of goin' down to the schoolhouse. Poker," he declared, working his lips in and out over toothless gums. "Now there's a game a man could sink his teeth into. Ain't that right, son?" he asked, spearing Tanner with a look.

Tanner stepped behind Jordan as if to use her as a shield. "Don't drag me into this."

"I ain't askin' you to play, boy. Just to agree. Man's gotta take a stand, else the womenfolk'll have it all their way. Best you learn that right off, 'specially in these early days of your marriage."

Jordan's head whipped around so fast, her hair smacked him in the face. "Marriage?" Stunned confusion colored the single word.

Hiram leaned forward in his chair, his spat with Thelma put on hold as he picked up on the undercurrents between the "newlyweds."

Tanner was more than happy to run damage control. He leaned down and covered her startled lips with his own. He felt the immediate softening, then resistance. Before she could do anything else to give them away, he pulled back and winked.

"Looks like I need to do a better job of helping you remember you're a new bride. Ready to head for the hotel?"

Her green eyes widened as she apparently caught on. "Oh. Don't be silly, darling. With Daddy so opposed to our marriage, I just hadn't realized you'd told anyone. Besides, I could never forget our wedding...or our wedding night."

Tanner shifted the grocery sacks to cover the effect her words had on his body. That sassy mouth kept surprising him. And if his arms hadn't been full, he'd have ended up causing a scandal, right here on the sidewalk in front of Thelma's general store.

The only thing that kept his control in check was her reference to her daddy's objections—which was more truth than fiction.

And despite his cloak of armor, the reminder hurt. Like the unsuitability of a marriage of Capulet and Montague, a Caldwell and Grazer union would never be accepted.

THEY WERE SITTING side by side on the floor of the kitchen and Jordan was having a hard time keeping her concentration on nursemaiding the puppies. Guilt ate at her over spending Tanner's money. In addition to the underwear, she'd bought a pair of sandals. Then, when it had come time to pay the vet's bill, he'd had to use a credit card—thank goodness the authorization had cleared.

Because of her, the man was going into debt.

"I appreciate you paying Dr. Eldon."

Tanner glanced up from trying to coax one of the puppies into drinking from a baby bottle. She noticed that the thigh of his jeans was wet from spilled milk. The sight made her heart give a jolt and she couldn't quite determine why.

"You got a fixation about money, Blackie?"

"No." Her own puppy whined when he lost his hold on the nipple. "But I prefer to pull my own weight. So far, you've been footing the bill for me."

"I did it for Annie."

The mother dog lay on a pile of blankets. She was anemic and fighting a low-grade infection, but Dr. Eldon had given her a shot of antibiotics and promised she'd regain her strength in a few days. In the meantime, though, she wasn't up to nursing her puppies.

"Yes, but the food and other stuff wasn't all for the dogs."

"I'm not broke." A note of censure crept into his voice.

Why did her worry keep coming across as an insult? She sighed and concentrated on the puppy in her lap, trying to keep her eyes and her mind off Tanner's capable, scarred hands ministering to the golden ball of fur that was sprawled across his thigh.

"It seems like every time I try to have a conversation with you, we end up wading through minefields. Neither one of us are the same people we were ten years ago. Would it be so terrible if we tried to get to know each other?"

"What do you want to know?"

She shrugged, trying to gather her thoughts. There were plenty of gaps, but she felt like she'd known him intimately all her life. It didn't make sense. Probably because she'd thought about him so often, spun so many fantasies about him.

"Where do you live?"

He seemed to hesitate. His thumb gently stroked between the puppy's ears. "Just outside Fresno."

"That's where your Mr. B. lives, isn't it?"

"Yeah."

"Well?"

"Well, what?"

If her hands weren't occupied with the puppy, she might have thrown something at him. "Ever had a conversation before?"

He scowled at her.

"It's a simple concept," she said, exasperated. "An exchange of information, pleasantries, the weather, whatever. It's more than one-word sentences."

Reluctantly, it seemed, his mouth canted at the corners. Brown eyes pinned her, full of amusement and something else she couldn't quite put a name to. He shook his head, shifting his long hair off his shoulders, then stretched his legs out against the tile floor, careful not to dislodge the sleeping puppy.

"Okay, we'll start over. Talk away and I'll try to hold up my end." Idly, his fingertip traced the pink belly of the little dog.

Now that he'd given her carte blanche, she wasn't sure where to start.

"Do you have pets?"

"No."

"Have you ever?" She couldn't imagine someone not surrounding themselves with animals. Animals never judged. They only loved. And they expected so little.

"No."

Her brow arched at his stingy syllables and he gave a soft chuckle.

"I'm not used to talking about myself."

"You'll get better at it. How come you never had a pet?"

"My old man wouldn't allow it. I brought home a stray cat once and he threatened to drown it."

"That's awful. Surely he didn't mean it?"

Tanner shrugged, remembering the fight that had turned physical and the poor scrawny cat hiding in the corner. He'd have given up anything to keep that animal.

"Douglas Caldwell wasn't what you'd call a prince of a man. I didn't want to take a chance that he was blowing smoke, so I found a good home for the stray." And had checked on it daily for more than a month, hiding behind a fence so no one would see him, see his longing, see the tough guy who lived in a squalid travel trailer mooning over an orange tabby.

Always on the outside…looking through the fence.

"I'm sorry," Jordan said, placing her sleeping puppy next to its mother. Annie lifted her head, nuzzled her offspring and turned weary, grateful eyes up to Jordan.

For a minute, Tanner wondered if she'd heard his thoughts. "It's no big deal. It was a long time ago."

"And what about now?"

"Now, I don't have a pet because I've been too busy to stay in one place for long. I haven't had the time to devote to an animal. I'd like to, though." He stroked the puppy in his lap, reluctant to move it just yet. "I'm thirty years old and I'd like to set down some roots. I'd always promised myself when I did that, I'd get a dog, maybe a few cats, some birds." He grinned. "Maybe even a snake."

As he'd known she would, she shuddered. "That'll keep me from visiting, for sure."

It felt as though his heart stood still for an instant. "You planning to visit with or without the husband?"

He saw the backtracking, saw the realization that she'd blurted out a platitude that had no ground in actuality. Saw the instant she remembered that their being here was only temporary, that kidnappers-at-large had forced her into this situation.

That her life was promised to another man.

"I… I—I meant…"

"I know what you meant, Blackie," he said softly. Her stammering reminded him of the sweet girl she'd been, the girl who rooted for the underdog—or the bad-boy misfit. "And I'll let you in on a secret. I'm not overly fond of snakes myself." To take that bruised look off her face—the look that suggested she was worrying about his feelings—he nodded to the puppy in his lap. "Decided on any names for these guys?"

"Why don't you decide?"

"I'm not good at that."

Jordan stared at him for several seconds, making a concentrated effort not to let her jaw drop. His quick denial held a host of undertones.

"Are you kidding? You call me Blackie because I've got black hair, and you call me duchess—which I object to, by the way—because you think I'm such a privileged miss. So take a good look at these little fur balls and come up with something."

He scowled at the puppies, then at her. For a minute she thought he was going to get up and leave the room.

"If I name them, it doesn't mean I'm keeping them."

"Why not? You said you wanted roots. Pets."

"I ride a Harley. I can't very well haul Annie and her runts on my bike."

The longing that came over him when he looked at the dogs was in direct contrast to his argumentative tone.

"What about the Jeep?"

"It belongs to Mr. B."

"I'll deliver them for you."

His gaze snapped to hers. "You and Russell?"

"Randall. And leave him out of this. I want a name."

Silence. Bordering on belligerence.

"Well?" she prompted.

"Buddy."

That surprised her. "Buddy?"

He looked embarrassed.

Jordan was charmed.

"What's wrong with Buddy?" His square jaw jutted out, and a strand of long hair caught on his beard stubble.

"Nothing. It's a good name. But it should mean something. What makes you think of him as Buddy?"

"Forget it." Despite his short tone, his hands were gentle as he laid the sleeping puppy next to its sibling. "It was a stupid idea."

"No. Tell me."

For the longest time, he stared at the abandoned mother and her offspring. His voice, when he spoke, was rough-edged and quiet. "I always wanted a pet because it would be my buddy." His tone gained strength, became dismissive. "But since I won't be keeping these, it's a dumb name."

She reached out and touched his arm. He reminded her of a little boy, embarrassed in front of his peers. "It's a perfect name. In fact, we'll call his brother Pal."

"No sense in going overboard, Blackie."

She made the mistake of looking into his eyes. And found herself trapped. Snared by his magnetism, his virility, the vulnerability he tried so hard to mask... Snared by her own desire.

Dear Lord, she wanted this man. Right there in the kitchen, sitting on the cold tile floor, surrounded by puppies.

Like an out-of-focus lens, her world gradually narrowed into crystal clarity, into just the two of them. Alone. No obligations. No outside forces to intrude.

Spellbound, she saw his hand lift, saw him move closer, felt his warm breath on her cheek.

For the life of her, she couldn't move.

Didn't want to move.

Restlessness stirred again. The desire to start something she had no business starting. Her heart pounded out of control, making her dizzy, weightless somehow...as though she were someone else.

As though she were free to take...and to give.

What could it hurt?

His lips were a mere breath away.

The voice of reason warred with passion. And for once, just this once, Jordan wanted to ignore the reason and go with the passion.

"So long," he whispered. "I've been waiting for you for so long."

"I know. Me, too. If you don't kiss me now, I think I'll go mad."

He cupped her face, closed his eyes and laid his forehead against hers. Jordan felt so confused. The urge to take nearly consumed her. Something held her back.

His features were tight, as though he were in pain. "Tanner?"

"We're in a hell of a fix, Blackie. If I don't kiss you, *you'll* go mad. If I do, *I'll* lose it."

"I don't understand."

"Neither do I. I have an idea I'm going to regret this until my dying day, but I think we should call it a night and go to bed." His lips brushed her brow. "Alone."

Chapter Nine

"I swear there's an epidemic," Tanner said.

Jordan rearranged the cardboard they'd fashioned to keep the puppies from running amok. Each day they were getting stronger, and more curious.

"An epidemic of what?" She'd been steering clear of Tanner as much as possible over the past week. If he hadn't gone all noble on her that night in the kitchen, they would have made love.

She still wanted to—with an increasing fervor that bordered on obsession.

"Botched weddings," Tanner said.

Jordan's heart lurched. For long periods of time, she was able to dismiss the danger from her mind. But then the restlessness would set in, the worry. With each day that passed without information, without an assurance that it was safe to go home, her fear increased. What if their whereabouts were found out and a genuine ransom was demanded? What if she didn't get back in time and the bank foreclosed on the estate? What if she returned to Grazer's Corners to find her stables empty, her stallion missing?

It was a nightmare that made it difficult to sleep.

"What's happened now?" There had been three weddings scheduled a week apart—Kate Bingham's, Jordan's, and Hailey Olson's to Garrett Keely.

"The details are sketchy, but according to Sonny, the bride didn't show and the groom came up missing."

"Garret? No way. The guy's a pro football player. He can definitely hold his own."

"Maybe with his fists."

"Are you saying there were more guns involved?" She didn't give him time to answer. "Lord, Tanner. What's happening to our town?"

"*Your* town," he corrected. "And I don't know the answer to either one of those questions."

"You think they were kidnapped, don't you?"

He shrugged. "They probably eloped."

"No. The Olsens would never stand still for that. I've got a bad feeling about this, Tanner. Do you think it's all tied together somehow? My situation, and Kate's, and now Garrett and Hailey's?"

"Not likely. Word is that Katie went of her own free will…like you did. For all we know, Garrett did, too."

"Kate Bingham went willingly?" Jordan had been so busy with her own plans—and her restlessness—that she hadn't kept tabs on the progress made with Kate's disappearance. That made her feel bad. She should have been more concerned.

And her willingness to stay with Tanner was another source of guilt.

"Seems so."

"The guy at the wedding," she mused, more to herself than as actual conversation. She remembered the fiasco, the handsome man who'd whisked Kate

out of harm's way. She also remembered that split
second, when she'd run to her daddy to make sure
he hadn't been hit by a stray bullet, an instant when
she'd glanced at the outlaw and seen his eyes connect with Kate's.

It was the type of look every female would recognize—the look of a man who wants a woman.

The same look she saw in Tanner's eyes.

"His name is Mitch Connery."

"Who?"

"The man Katie went off with. And he's wanted
for murder."

Jordan drew in a breath. "She went willingly with
a man who's wanted for murder?"

"I don't imagine she knew it at the time. And
you're not in a great position to cast stones—"

"I wasn't casting stones," she interrupted, then
frowned. "Why?"

"Because you went with me without knowing
anything about me."

"I knew enough."

"Enough to be afraid?"

"I'm not afraid of you."

"You should be."

"Because you want to make love with me?"

Her bluntness apparently took him by surprise.
His hand jerked as he reached for the coffeepot.
Glass clinked against hard plastic so sharply, it was
a wonder the carafe didn't shatter. "Don't go there,
Blackie."

Her heart slammed into its runaway-gallop mode.
Around Tanner, that seemed to be a common oc-
currence. It was a testament to her good health that
she hadn't keeled over from a stroke yet.

And as much as she knew she shouldn't be pursuing this conversational avenue, she couldn't seem to stop herself. "Would it be so wrong?"

"Are you willing to give up your plans for marriage?"

She knew that guilt, as well as her answer, was written on her face.

"Ah," he said. "The rich girl looking for a secret fling."

His nasty words stung, and she felt tears well, felt her throat ache. She wanted to tell him that it wouldn't be a fling, that he meant much more to her. So much more.

What had started out as a girlhood crush, had matured into something much more powerful.

Something that felt a lot like love.

But with regard to Tanner, that wasn't an emotion she was at liberty to examine, to allow to blossom, to hope for.

Turning her back to him, she stared down at Buddy and Pal, who were curled trustingly against Annie's belly.

Would she ever have anyone of her own with whom she could curl up so comfortably? A dim image of Randall popped into her mind and she shook her head. Randall didn't inspire feelings of protectiveness, or of safety.

But Tanner did. And that hurt, because he was the wrong man.

After swallowing back the pain over what could not be, she at last found her voice. "I'm sorry," she whispered. "I'm not being fair. I don't blame you for thinking I'm nothing more than a shallow debutante."

She hadn't realized he'd moved behind her until he laid a gentle hand on her shoulder, and turned her to face him.

"No. I'm the one who's sorry. You're not shallow, Jordan." His knuckles lightly grazed her cheek. "I'm starting to realize that the layers of you go fathoms deep."

"Maybe to the wrong depths, though."

"Why's that?"

She closed her eyes. Like an ostrich with its head in the sand, she'd avoided dwelling on her reasons for marrying Randall, hadn't spent a lot of time analyzing the right and wrong of marrying for money. Now, it seemed, that was all she could think about. "Never mind."

He held her in place, his hands gentle on her shoulders. The clock above the dinette table ticked like a time bomb in the silence.

"Do you love Latrobe?"

"He's a good man."

"That's not what I asked."

"I know, but if I answer you honestly, you'll misunderstand."

"Try me."

This would be like negotiating through a minefield. She hadn't forced herself to think too closely about her relationship with Randall.

Until Tanner had come back into her life.

"I care a great deal for Randall. He's ambitious, and he's good to me. But I don't feel a burning passion for him."

She saw the way Tanner's eyes flared.

"See? I knew you'd misunderstand." She pulled away, and crossed her arms over her chest. "You're thinking that because I don't get all hot and bothered with Randall, I'm wanting to use you as a substitute. And that's just not so."

"So, I make you all hot and bothered?"

There was no accusation in his tone as she might have expected. Only curiosity. Sexy curiosity.

"I honestly think I should plead the fifth on that."

"Plead all you want. The truth is in your eyes. Answer me something, though."

She nodded. "If I can."

"Is there more to it than just hormones?"

She couldn't hold his gaze. Especially because she'd just decided she owed him total honesty. "Yes. Much more. But that's as far as I can let it go. I made a promise, Tanner. When it's safe to go home, I have to marry Randall."

THE YAP AND WHINE of the puppies woke her. Pulling on the loose cotton shorts under her T-shirt, she made her way into the kitchen, and stopped at the sight she saw.

With only the light over the stove for illumination, Tanner sat on the floor, talking softly to Pal, who was drinking from the baby bottle, milk dribbling down the sides of his furry mouth. Buddy gamboled nearby, attempting to climb into Tanner's lap, yet the puppy didn't quite have the agility, or the height, to accomplish the feat. Annie looked on in appreciative adoration, her black-and-white muzzle resting on Tanner's thigh.

"I've only got two hands, Buddy," he said to the whining puppy. "You'll have to wait your turn."

Butterflies took wing in Jordan's stomach. As much as she tried to stretch her imagination, she just couldn't picture Randall sitting on a kitchen floor conversing with puppies. And although she knew it was dangerous to continually compare Randall with Tanner, she couldn't seem to help herself.

Unwilling to disturb him yet, she stayed just inside the kitchen doorway and watched. He looked so tough sitting there, wearing only a pair of jeans, his long, dark hair falling across his bare shoulders. With his head bent, his hair nearly reached his nipples.

She wanted to touch him there—his chest, that rock-hard stomach—wanted to map his body with her hands, shower him with kisses, commit every part of him to her memory. A memory she could take out and examine when they were no longer together.

The desire that spiraled through her was near agony. She cleared her throat and his head snapped up.

"Need some help?" she asked, pleased that her voice actually worked.

His eyes held hers, riveting her to the spot. She saw his gaze shift to her hair, then to her T-shirt where she knew her nipples stood out against the cotton. Although the light was dim, she had an idea he knew the state her body was in. She could see it in his gaze—especially when it lingered on the hem of her shorts.

Shorts that she wore without underwear.

Pal lost his hold on the bottle and whined. The sound had Annie lifting her head in apparent disapproval and Buddy yapping anew.

"I thought I could get to them before they woke you," Tanner said softly. "I hadn't counted on Buddy being such an impatient little squirt."

Jordan smiled, and Tanner nearly forgot what he was supposed to be doing. Her jet-black hair was sleep-tousled and sexy as hell. The T-shirt she wore almost covered her shorts, but still, those long, bare legs were igniting his fantasies.

By damn, he was restless. He wasn't used to somebody else handling investigations, and he'd had to stop himself from calling Sonny every five minutes. That would blow the other man's cover and they'd never find out who was threatening Jordan.

The way he was feeling right now, though, Tanner figured it would be safer all around if *he* was in Grazer's Corners and Sonny was guarding Jordan.

He didn't know how much longer he could keep his hands off her.

When she eased down next to him, he caught a whiff of the shampoo scent that clung to her hair, and his body reacted with typical speed.

Hell on fire, he was tired of fighting it—of fighting these reactions. Tired of playing fair.

She scooped up Buddy, and used the cabinets for a backrest as he was doing.

"How come we always end up on the floor?" she asked.

"I don't know. But I can think of much better things to do down here than bottle-feeding puppies."

Her hand jerked and her hair swished across her shoulders. "Be good."

"I guarantee you, I will be." For the life of him, he didn't know why he was baiting her. *He'd* been the one running, the one to call a halt when things heated up. In the deep of the night, though, in the shadowy light of the stove, the banter somehow felt right.

Especially when she flashed him that sassy grin. Damned if he didn't appreciate the woman she'd grown up to be.

"Evidently you're feeling pretty safe since we have the babies to take care of," she teased.

"Evidently."

Pal had about had his fill and was only toying with the rubber nipple. Tanner set the bottle on the floor, and Annie gave it a sniff as though checking how much was left. He could have put the fluffy puppy back in its makeshift box, but it felt good to cuddle it. Besides, it gave him something to do with his hands, kept him from reaching out to run his fingertips beneath the hem of Jordan's shorts, just to satisfy his curiosity about whether or not she was wearing panties.

The problem was, his curiosity wouldn't stop there. And he knew exactly where the quest would lead; knew, too, that she would let him.

But that would only start them on a journey that would dead-end all too soon. And the only road he wanted to travel with Jordan was a road that led unencumbered into the future.

The wall clock over the dinette set ticked rhythmically as the second hand moved around the dial. Pressure built in his chest.

"Earlier, you said that you *had* to get married. Are you pregnant?"

Her burst of laughter startled the puppies. "No."

"Then why are you marrying Latrobe?"

"He asked, I said yes." She shrugged as though that should be the end of it. "I gave my word."

"There's more to it than making a promise."

"I never go back on my word."

Her adamance set off warning signals in his brain. "That's admirable, Blackie, but don't you think you're carrying a vow too far? Especially since it'll affect the rest of your life?"

"I can't back out."

He frowned. "There's that word again. Can't. There's more that you're not saying."

"There wasn't before *you* came along."

He knew she hadn't meant to admit that, and he wasn't going to let her get out of it or take the words back. "Explain."

She looked everywhere but at him. "The puppies are sleeping.... I should go back to bed."

He gripped her wrist to hold her still. "Uh-uh. Tell me what my coming along has to do with anything."

She let out a resigned breath. "You make me *feel*."

He skimmed a finger over her arm. "Feel what?"

"Special..." His fingertip worked its way down to her hand. She turned her palm up, linked her fingers with his. "Desire."

"You've already told me it's more than lust."

"Yes. I can't define it, though. It's not..."

"Right?" he finished when her words trailed off.

She released a pent-up sigh. "The way you make me feel is terribly unfair to Randall."

"Which brings us back to the original question. Why are you marrying him? It's not as though you wouldn't have a ton of other prospects."

"Thank you." She traced her thumb over the scar at his knuckle. He made her feel so many things—

made her want. His interest in her was genuine, and that was something special. Too many times in her life, people had sought out her company because of who she was—Maynard Grazer's daughter.

With Tanner, though, it was different. And in the quiet of the night, with his fingers twined warmly, solidly with hers, admission came easily.

"Daddy's having financial troubles. Once the south vineyards yield, we should be okay, but in the meantime, he needs a loan to carry him through. It's a well-guarded secret that he's not as solvent as people think. On paper, though, there isn't a bank that will touch his application."

"Except Randall's."

She nodded. "It's political. Linking mine and Randall's name will look good on the application. He can push the paperwork through."

"So, you're collateral?"

She sucked in a breath. "It's not like that. We were engaged before the loan came up."

"I don't get it, Jordan. Surely money isn't that important. Not compared to tying yourself to someone you don't love."

"I never said I didn't love him."

"You never said that you did, either."

The dissension welled in her again, the restlessness. How could she explain to him that she didn't have a choice? At least, not one she could comfortably live with. No matter what Tanner made her feel, no matter what she felt—or didn't feel—for Randall, she wasn't free to back out of the marriage.

"Daddy has always given me everything I could ever want. Maybe somehow I feel responsible for his shaky finances."

"That's bull and you know it."

"No, I don't. I need to do my part, Tanner. For Daddy...and for my horses."

"The horses?"

"The stables are part of the estate. If Daddy loses the house, we lose the stables, too."

"I thought you were planning to take the horses with you after your marriage."

"Eventually. Randall wants to be certain they're a sound investment before he follows through and builds stables."

"He'll guarantee a loan that's not a sound investment, yet he won't take a chance on you? On your goals and abilities?"

"Daddy has a track record."

"Not a very good one, obviously."

"I know there's no love lost between the two of you, but Daddy's a good man."

"Like Latrobe." He gave a low snort. "I don't know, Blackie, it sounds to me like the two men in your life have a habit of letting you down, not giving you enough credit."

"Daddy's never let me down," she defended.

"He supports your dream?"

"Yes." Mostly.

"Does your father foot the bill for the stables?"

"He did in the beginning. Now, it pretty much pays for itself. But it's still more of a break-even proposition. It'll be at least another year before I'll realize any sizable profits." She took a breath, trying to clear away the building tension. "I'm tired of taking, Tanner. It's time I gave something back. And Randall will be a good husband."

"Keep repeating that and maybe you'll convince yourself."

She closed her eyes, forgot to guard her words. "I wouldn't need to convince myself if you hadn't come back."

He leaned forward, turned her face toward his. His eyes were intent, serious. "Don't do it, baby. Don't throw your life away."

"I'm not. I just wish…"

"What?"

She shook her head. "That things were different. That *we* were different."

"That I wasn't from the wrong side of the tracks?"

It shouldn't have made a difference, but it did in her family's eyes. Her family wouldn't accept a union like theirs. And she shouldn't even be thinking about them as a couple in the first place. Too many people were counting on her to do the right thing.

"I'm sorry," she whispered. "That attitude is so wrong. I hate it. But I don't know how to change it, to change my father. I've never thought of you that way, Tanner."

"Shh. Easy, baby. I know. You're good clear through to the inside. So rare."

When his lips touched hers, something close to desperation burst within Jordan. She wanted to rest against him, to climb right inside him, to be the woman of this man's heart.

Her fingers trembled as she touched his smooth, bare chest. How many times had she dreamed of this? Of being held, of having the freedom to caress. To explore.

The muscles beneath his sleek skin were well-defined, so powerful. And even as she felt them bunch and flex, she knew his strength would never harm her. He represented safety, and longing…and love.

There was magic to be had in Tanner's arms. And she wanted that magic, even if it was only for a day or a week, or simply mere minutes.

The wanting was like a storm raging inside her. Maybe it was wrong. But the pull was too strong.

There had been three possible kidnapping attempts in her hometown. Guns had been waved around. Threats had been made. Life as she'd known it no longer existed. There were no safe zones.

Except with Tanner.

He made her feel cherished.

He owned her heart.

That in itself put her in danger, but right now, she was willing to test that danger, to step into the storm and ignore the consequences. Who knew what would happen tomorrow? What life would hold? And because of that uncertainty, she could no longer deny herself—deny what they might share together.

She shifted against him, buried her hands in his long, silky hair.

"I just want the world to go away, Tanner." Although desire spiraled, inexplicably, she wanted to weep. "Make love with me. I don't want to hurt you, but…"

"The only thing that'll hurt me right now is if I can't have you. I've wanted you for so long, baby."

"I never knew." His words bolstered her, and she wound her arms around his neck. "It'll be enough, won't it?" She needed to convince herself as well as him. She wasn't making promises; she'd already made those. To another man. And maybe that was a mistake, but it was done.

It might well break her heart, but she couldn't stop herself from wanting Tanner. She needed him. Needed this. Once. For herself.

Soon enough she'd go back to thinking about everyone else's needs.

Tonight, she selfishly decided, was for *her* needs.

Tanner stood and lifted her into his arms. It seemed like he'd waited a lifetime to touch her like this, to hold her. He felt his arms tremble, and knew it wasn't from the exertion of carrying her. He could have carried twice her weight without breaking into a sweat.

"I don't know if it'll be enough, baby. I'm willing to give it a try, though. To find out."

He wanted to beg her for promises, but knew he couldn't. So, he'd take what she could give, for the moment. Just for this moment.

In his bedroom, he set her on her feet by the bedside and switched on the lamp. The sheets were tangled from his restless attempt at sleep before the puppies had given him an excuse to get up.

He saw her gaze shift to the mattress, then back to him, saw the hesitation in the way she licked her lips.

He'd expected cool grace when he got her in bed. He hadn't expected innocence.

"Don't go shy on me now."

Her lips trembled. "I think I'm a little scared."

The admission charmed Tanner right down to his soul. "That makes two of us. I'm a lot scared."

"You? I wouldn't think anything could scare you."

"You do." With a single finger, he traced her throat, then ran his palm over the well-washed material of the T-shirt, cupping her breast through the cotton. Wanting to linger, afraid he'd rush, he gripped the hem of the shirt and slowly drew it over her head.

Wind rustled the leaves outside, carrying the scent of the lake through the open window. Tanner drew in a breath, inhaling the smell of nature and of Jordan. She was like a vision that he was afraid to touch, afraid she'd vanish.

"I knew you'd be perfect."

Jordan nearly closed her eyes, but she didn't want to miss a second of what was about to happen, didn't want to miss anything about Tanner. The reverence in his quiet words rocked her unsteady foundation as nothing else could have.

A delicious quiver of excitement spiraled through her as he simply watched her. The heat of his gaze was like a physical touch.

"There's nothing perfect about me." But he made her feel that way.

"Let me be the judge of that."

He spent a long moment tracing her lips with his, then moved lower—gently, reverently—cupping her breasts in his hands, sending her soaring. Her knees nearly buckled when his lips and tongue replaced his hands.

She grabbed his shoulders for balance, arched into him.

"Easy." He moved upward to meet her gaze again.

She made a frustrated sound deep in her throat

and wrapped her arms around him, pressing her breasts to his bare chest. Skin to skin, the friction was almost too much.

Desire whipped through her like a hot desert wind as he cupped her bottom and pulled her firmly against him. She felt his fingertips like a brand through the thin barrier of cotton.

"Oh, Tanner...hurry."

His fingers hooked in the waistband of her shorts. "No way, baby. None of us know what tomorrow will bring. We're gonna make this last." He sucked in a breath when she at last stood naked before him. "The reality's better than the fantasy."

"What?" She could hardly think. His steady, intense gaze absorbed her, made her burn and throb and ache.

"You. Naked. It's been pure torture watching you this past week, that sweet body covered by cotton...without a stitch on underneath. You don't know how many times I've wanted to peel those shorts off you."

"I bought underwear."

"Yeah, but the damage had been done. I still imagined the way you looked in my shorts, without panty lines...and no bra." He cupped her breasts, his eyes going impossibly dark. He looked sexy and dangerous, so unconventional with all that swinging hair; like a warrior, a conqueror.

Through hot, intense eyes that gave away little of what he was thinking or feeling, he watched her, thrilling her.

Her heart pumped and her mouth went dry as dust. This was what she'd been waiting for—a man who looked at her just this way, with a heated gaze so compelling, so powerful, so exclusive, it might well have been a physical touch.

His gaze shifted, in a slow, thorough once-over, from the top of her head to the tips of her bare toes. Like a raging firestorm, it swept a path of licking flames, leaving her exquisitely sensitized.

And if a mere look was that powerful, she could hardly imagine what those big, strong, scarred hands would be like.

Touching her all over. Arousing her.

She didn't have a lot of experience with men, could count her intimate relationships on the fingers of one hand. Again, as she had a week and a half ago at the bar, she had to wonder if she was woman enough to handle this man.

One thing was for certain—she was determined to find out. Soon. Before she turned into a quivering puddle at his feet from the scorch of his sensual gaze.

"I have this fantasy," he murmured, his voice low and rough.

Her heart quaked. Yet, for the life of her, she couldn't find her voice.

"I'd like for you to dance for me...like you did that night at Gatlin's."

Embarrassment flared, flushing her cheeks. Or was it desire?

"But I think we'll leave that for another time," he said. "I don't think I could last." His lips lightly grazed hers.

Wanting more, *needing* more, she leaned into him.

"You're the only woman who's ever occupied so many of my thoughts, my fantasies."

Her breath was coming faster now. "That's only

because we're isolated out here. There's just the two of us.''

"Not just this past week. For ten years, every time I close my eyes, it's you I see.'' He hadn't meant to admit that. It made him vulnerable. To cover the slip, he jerked her to him, more roughly than he should have.

For an instant he went absolutely still, alert to every nuance of her body language. If she'd indicated by so much as a twitch that he'd frightened her, he would have let her go.

But she surprised him again, meeting his aggression with a greedy avidness of her own, rubbing against him, pressing as though she couldn't bear to have even a layer of skin separating them. Sweet, seductive moans rose from deep in her throat.

They set him on fire.

She wasn't a hothouse flower to be handled with kid gloves, yet he wanted to treat her that way, give her only gentle touches and stoke the fires slowly, easily.

She took the decision from him, though, grabbing the waistband of his jeans, working the buttons even as she dragged him down with her on the bed.

He chuckled when their legs and hands tangled, surprising himself. He couldn't recall ever feeling the desire to laugh with a woman while they were in bed. "Hold it a sec, Blackie.''

"I'm trying,'' she said, slipping her hands inside his pants, pushing them down. "You're not cooperating.''

His shout of laughter was muffled against her neck. "Shameless.''

"I repeat, I'm trying.'' Jordan made an effort to curb her urgency. She smoothed her palms up his chest, then tunneled her fingers in his hair, cupping his face, holding him back for just a minute so she could enjoy that sexy dimple that winked in his cheek.

As she gazed into his velvety brown eyes, amusement shifted, heated. Eyes open, steady, he lowered his head, his lips touching hers so gently, yet she felt their power rush through her veins, from the roots of her hair to the soles of her feet.

Her heart quaked in anticipation once more, like a teapot simmering, about to boil. He was a beautiful, virile man.

And for tonight, he was all hers.

A sudden wave of desperation crashed over her and she wrapped her arms around him as urgency built. Like the fragment of a dream that materializes out of nowhere, she realized she'd been subconsciously waiting for him for most of her life.

"Make love with me, Tanner."

"All night, baby." His voice lowered to a whisper, roughening with a thrilling, excruciatingly sensual promise. "But there're a few fantasies I want to take care of first...other than the solo dance."

His tongue traced the ultrasensitive spot just behind her ear, then slid lower, and lower still, covering every inch of flesh on her body.

He savored, feasted, drove her mad. Her heart pumped and her hands fisted against the sheets as his flowing hair brushed against her thighs. When his lips settled over her in a shockingly intimate kiss, she nearly cannoned off the bed.

"So sweet," he murmured.

She had a fleeting thought about the raw emotion in his voice, the absolute sincerity, as though she were the most cherished prize a man could wish for.

But her mind went blank of everything except the wild, incendiary explosion that suddenly consumed her.

Release shuddered through her, again and again, dizzying and glorious.

Her nails dug into his shoulders as she tugged, panting. "Now...no more."

He seemed to understand her plea, a plea that even to her own ringing ears made no sense. All she knew at this point was that she wanted. Fiercely. Wildly.

He rose above her like a tender warrior, his brown eyes blazing with heat, dark hair framing his face and shoulders. So unconventional...so absolutely perfect.

Her breath caught at the look in his eyes—a look of possession, a look of love.

No! she nearly screamed. *Don't fall in love with me. One of us with a broken heart is more than enough.* But the words remained locked in her throat as he eased up her body, and joined them as one.

He filled her completely, clear through to her soul. She hadn't known—oh, she'd had no idea—that it could get better. The friction of his thrusts set off sparks of incredible sensation that burst through her in a powerful, pounding climax.

And all she could do was hold him, meet his fervor, seeking an anchor, any anchor, in the turbulent storm that quickly spun out of control, giving her the rarest glimpse of what could only have been paradise.

Chapter Ten

With her heart still pounding against his chest, Jordan curled next to Tanner, feeling giddy, and yet fragile. What they had just shared had rocked her world.

And the fact that they were on borrowed time, that he wasn't hers to hold, made her want to weep.

But now was not the time for tears. Seconds were precious. The world could wait for a while. For the time being, she could dream.

"You're a fraud, Tanner Caldwell."

He jolted. "Excuse me?"

"You like to give the impression you're a tough guy, but you're gentle."

His dimples flashed. Chills chased across her skin as his fingertips feathered over her arm. "If what we just did felt gentle to you, maybe I'm losing my touch. It took damn near everything out of me."

His chest was damp beneath the caress of her palm. Strands of his long hair clung to his neck.

"Your technique is definitely not in question, so put a rein on that ego." She patted the firm skin above where his heart still beat rapidly. "I meant inside. You have a good heart, yet sometimes you give the impression that you're mad at the world. I imagine it makes people scared to approach you."

"That's something I learned the hard way." His voice was hushed, as though to speak louder would disturb the stillness of the night, the isolation of just the two of them, alone among the mussed sheets of the bed.

"Growing up as poor white trash, I had to fight for everything—even the right to walk through certain parts of town. I got to be pretty good with my fists, which was a bonus after I left Grazer's Corners. It takes attitude to live on the streets."

She drew in a swift breath. "You were homeless?"

"For a while." A gentle breeze fluttered the curtains over the open window, bringing with it the sound of a night bird calling to its mate. "When my old man took off, there was nothing left for me here. I hitched my way to San Francisco. That chip on my shoulder you're so fond of picking on saved me more than once."

"I imagine it caused you some grief, too."

"Some. I got in plenty of street fights, gained a reputation as a tough guy. That suited my purposes," he admitted. "But the anger and the fire made the desire to *be* somebody burn even hotter."

"You've always been somebody."

He kissed the top of her head, her fierce defense of him taking some of the sting out of his memories. Memories of the uglier side of human nature that a sheltered woman like Jordan would know nothing about. Or shouldn't, anyhow. If they couldn't pinpoint the identity of the kidnappers, she'd likely get a fast education. No, he promised himself. Not as long as he was around. If it took all his time and considerable money, he'd make sure she was safe.

"What happened then? What turned you around?"

"Who said I've been turned around?"

She thumped him lightly on the chest.

He grinned and captured her hand, kissing her knuckles. "I saved an eccentric millionaire from being mugged and earned myself a job as bodyguard."

"Mr. B.?"

"Yeah." He said the word softly and with deep affection. "He's the best thing that ever happened to me. Became a sort of surrogate father to me—the type of father I'd always wanted."

"And your own father?"

"Dead. Jackknifed the travel trailer and wrapped the pickup around a tree. Drunk, as usual."

"I'm sorry."

He shrugged, yet held her just a little tighter. "It was bound to happen sooner or later."

"But it hurt."

"I suppose." Even through the shame, he'd loved that old man. For the life of him, he couldn't figure out why.

"So, what's it like being a bodyguard to a millionaire?"

"Bloodthirsty little thing, aren't you?" He smiled when he felt her bristle. "It's not as exciting and violence-ridden as you're probably imagining."

"Obviously I don't know much about bodyguards." She sniffed, settling against him. "Other than what you've done for me."

His long hair shifted against the pillow, mingling with hers as he turned his head, looking down at her. "I assure you, baby, guarding your body is way different than anything I did for Mr. B."

Her surprised chuckle was muffled against his shoulder. "You're bad."

"Yes. I can be." He said it teasingly, yet there was a more literal undertone that he couldn't ignore—a life-style that was ingrained in him, that would probably shock her right down to her sexy toes if he told her all the gritty details.

"Anyway," he said, dragging his mind to more pleasant thoughts, "I didn't spend all my time standing around flexing muscles and looking mean. Mr. B. has a thing for collecting gadgets. At the time, his latest passion was computers, but he didn't know anything about them. I was game to learn and he encouraged me to tinker. It didn't take long for us to realize I had a natural aptitude for them. I spent hours hacking on those machines, going deeper and deeper into their workings, so amazed at the capabilities." It sneaked up on him sometimes, this exhilaration that engulfed him, that could get him so wound up on a subject.

"Those babies were limitless. And so was I, evidently—limitless and relentless. I turned into one of those eggheads."

She gave an indelicate snort. "Sorry, Tanner, I can't quite get that image to gel. With your long hair and tough body, you don't look anything like the stereotypical nerd."

His ego took a healthy leap at the admiration shining from her green eyes. "Thanks for the compliment."

"You're welcome." Absently, she gave his chest a quick kiss. "Continue."

His body went absolutely still. Having her full attention focused on the deeper layers of his life, of the things that mattered, was exciting. But his sudden need to have her focus on a *different* part of him was fast making its presence known. "This communication thing is wearing me out. Sure you want to keep talking?"

"Mmm-hmm."

The lazy way her tongue circled his nipple made concentration next to impossible. His own hands smoothed over her hips, then rested on her firm bottom.

"The intricacies of computer technology grabbed me by the throat and wouldn't let go. It became an obsession." He cupped the soft curve of her buttocks, teasing, stroking, squeezing. "And although I didn't have 'the look'—as you put it—I had the aptitude..." His voice sounded hoarse even to his own ears. "And the drive."

"Obsession can be a good thing...." Her breathing wasn't quite as steady now. Her hand trailed down his belly, skimmed his thighs, coming scant inches from the part of him that was hard and aching for her touch. "Definitely have the drive," she murmured. "Go on."

"You're a vixen." In a swift move that made her breath catch, he hauled her on top of him, aligning their bodies in a way that both teased and thrilled.

"When Mr. B.'s fortress was breached, I designed a surveillance program that even the most sophisticated burglar couldn't penetrate—a high-tech sensor controlled by the computers." She'd given him the perfect opportunity to fess up over the size of his bank account, to tell her that with backing from Mr.

B., he'd patented the security program and made a fortune.

Instead, every sane thought went right out of his head when she shifted against him, pressing, rubbing, driving him mad.

"Smart man."

"Yeah, and a smart man knows when to shut up and concentrate on more important matters."

Jordan felt her smile blossom—slowly, brilliantly, bathing her insides with joy and wicked anticipation. Breeze from the open window whispered over her sensitized skin. The racket of frogs and insects, and the echo of an owl over the lake gave her world a surreal ambience.

Oh, it was so easy to forget about everyone and everything outside this bedroom, so easy to dream.

So easy to love.

Her hands tightened on his shoulders and her heart leaped with a painful thudding. Could he see the truth in her eyes?

The hopelessness of that truth?

The bittersweet reminder sent a stinging rush through her blood. She closed her eyes, pressed her mouth to his, her urgency building, nearly consuming her. She poured everything she possessed, body and soul, into the kiss, angling her head for better access, holding on.

Skin to skin, restlessly, she moved against him, telling him without words that he had her heart, apologizing with the brush of her lips that she couldn't give him more.

Like a sign of impending doom, an eerie sensation swept over her, closing her throat, spilling tears over her lids.

Tanner tunneled his fingers through her hair, holding her back, searching her eyes.

"Baby...shh. What's wrong?"

The concern in his voice and in his gentle brown eyes made her unsteady emotions sharper, like the blade of a razor slicing her heart into pieces.

She shook her head, unable to tell him that she wanted him for a lifetime, yet could only allow the moment.

"I want you," she whispered, settling for the understatement.

"And you've got me. All night." He shifted her beneath him, brushed his thumb over her damp cheeks. "Don't cry, sweetheart."

She gave a watery chuckle. "I'm not."

His brow arched. She knew he wanted an explanation. But she couldn't give it. Instead, she drew him down to her, closed her teeth gently over his lobe, reveled in the tickle of his long hair against her breasts.

"You make me feel so full, Tanner. Like I'll simply burst," she whispered.

"And that makes you cry?" He sounded so confused, so out of his depth.

She smiled. "Yes. Pretty dumb, huh?"

"No. Not dumb." His lips rested against her brow for a long moment. "Scary, though." He rose up a couple of inches, searched her features. "You sure they're...like, happy tears?"

Thankfully she had herself back under control. "Mmm-hmm. But they're about to turn into frustrated tears if you don't make a move fairly soon."

That sexy dimple flashed, and the look he gave her was so hot it was a wonder their bodies didn't steam. "You were doing a pretty good job of making the moves a few minutes ago."

"Well, I certainly thought so…until a certain macho guy decided he needed to call the shots."

"You want to be on top?"

"It felt pretty good up there."

Twin dimples now. Eyes twinkling like the devil. "Yeah. It felt pretty good. Next time," he promised.

"Next time, what?" Drawing a decent breath was becoming difficult. His clever hands and lips were busy.

"Next time we'll try it your way. Right now it seems I've got an obligation to uphold."

For the life of her, she couldn't seem to follow his logic. Could be it had something to do with the wildly sensual thing he was doing to her ear with his tongue. Or the fact that his finger had just slipped inside her. Her breath snagged, then left in a rush.

"Wh-what obligation?" she panted. Her stomach pulled deeply as pleasure spiraled, robbing her words and her sanity.

"To show you my moves. Hold on tight, baby. This is gonna take a good long while."

And it did, each exquisite moment taking her higher and higher. In shocking, thrilling, erotically earthshaking detail, Tanner Caldwell showed her the difference between routine lovemaking and the dangerously addictive touch of a rebel.

WHEN TANNER WOKE UP alone, he nearly panicked. What had possessed him to unleash his control the way he had? Man alive, he'd probably scared the hell out of her.

He yanked on his jeans and didn't bother with a shirt.

But before he could make it out of the room, the cell phone rang.

He snatched it up and punched in the code. "Caldwell."

A deep chuckle came over the line. "Catch you at a bad time, son?"

"No." *Yes.* Senses going on alert, he sank onto the mattress. If there was a need to apologize for his ardor, it would have to wait. "What's up, Mr. B.?"

"Well, all hell's broke loose out here."

Tanner frowned, his tension inching up another notch. "Out here? Where are you?"

"In Grazer's Corners. And before you get all uppity, I'll tell you that I've been in constant contact with Sonny."

A smile tugged. He'd known Samuel Bartholomew wouldn't sit on the sidelines for long. "Okay. What have you got for me?"

"Good news and bad."

"Go with the bad first."

"Maynard Grazer's in the hospital. Looks like a heart attack."

Tanner swore. The promise of a hundred top-of-the-line Thoroughbreds wouldn't keep Jordan away from town—and possible danger—now. "Bad one?"

"Docs aren't telling yet. They haven't actually given a diagnosis. Could be all the stress from what's been going on—his little girl missing, and all."

"Okay, we'll get back to that in a minute. Give me the good stuff. And it better be something to do with it being safe for me to bring Jordan back home. This isn't something I can keep from her, and I can guarantee you she won't sit still.''

''Patience, my boy. Sonny got a fix on the license plate of the van that followed you out of town. Took a while to track it down because the new owners didn't transfer the registration. Belongs to a couple of fellows out of Oregon—Cyrus and Alvin Smally. Maynard Grazer's uncle and cousin by marriage.'' He paused. ''Looks like the old man was in on it all along. Want me to notify the authorities?''

For the first time in as long as he could remember, Tanner was struck speechless. He'd commented to Jordan about Maynard being a suspect. He'd been grabbing at straws, talking from his own raw emotions where that man was concerned. He hadn't actually thought…

''Are the Smallys still around?''

''Uh, no.'' Mr. B. Cleared his throat. ''Sonny *persuaded* them it wouldn't be healthy to remain.''

And Sonny was very skilled at that sort of thing. ''Did they actually name Grazer? Give any reasons? Details?'' Granted, Maynard wasn't one of Tanner's favorite people, but Jordan cared. News like this would devastate her.

For her sake, he wanted to find a kernel of doubt.

''They said 'the boss' and 'the broad's family.'''

Tanner winced. ''Close enough. You say you're there? In Grazer's Corners?''

''Right here at the ranch. I figured it was safe. And I did want to have a look-see myself. Besides, you know Sonny. He's got itchy feet, won't stay anywhere a second longer than necessary.'' Samuel paused, his tone becoming concerned. ''I'm worried about him. He's not bouncing back from his wife's and baby's deaths.''

Tanner could have made a reference to pots calling kettles black, but he refrained. It had taken Samuel Bartholomew thirty years to recover from losing Ellie.

Somebody ought to do a study, he thought. All the literature dealt with how a woman could get over losing her man. In Tanner's personal experience— Mr. B., Sonny and himself included—it was the men who suffered the most from a loss.

Technically, Jordan had never been his to lose, but he'd suffered nonetheless. And now, after coming so close, after actually tasting the sweet promise of his dream, he knew he wouldn't recover any time soon.

He also knew there was a very good chance he was about to lose her. Once they were back in Grazer's Corners, the playing field would change.

He tried to keep his mind focused on Jordan's safety.

''What's your opinion of Grazer?'' Tanner asked, feeling sick to his stomach that a father might actually arrange for his own daughter to be kidnapped. But he valued Samuel's opinion and wanted to hear it, forced himself to keep an open mind.

''He loves the girl. That much is clear. If he *did* hire the goons, it was a mistake. A mistake he's paying for with his health.''

''Then it's safe for her to return?''

''Yes, I honestly believe so. Only a fool would try a stunt like this a second time, and frankly, Grazer doesn't strike me as a fool.''

Why did his heart feel as though it had a huge

hole in the center? A hole that was getting wider by the second?

This was what they'd wanted, what they were waiting for. The all-clear message. But Tanner's brain screamed that it was too soon. He needed more time; he didn't want to share her or give her up. But that was selfish thinking on his part. Her father's health was at risk. Now was not the time to pressure her. And ultimately, if there was to be any sort of relationship between them, the decision would have to be Jordan's.

"Okay. We'll pack up and be there later this morning."

"I'll wait for you here at Grazer's ranch."

Tanner ended the call, his unfocused gaze riveted on the mussed sheets of the bed. And that reminded him that Jordan was missing. He'd expected to wake up beside her—especially after the night they'd shared.

He'd had an entirely different plan in mind for this morning, had imagined starting all over again. With her toes this time, and working his way up.

Now he had to give her the news of her father— the partial news, anyway.

He left the bedroom, shutting his mind to the bed and the activities he'd like to engage in there. When he stepped into the kitchen, his feet felt as though they were rooted in cement.

Everything within him stilled at the sight before him. His heart should have felt light; instead it felt like a bowling ball in his chest.

Impressions flashed one right after another— dawn in the fragile stillness, songbirds singing outside, a beautiful woman cuddling warm puppies, her green eyes lighting up as he came into the room.

It didn't get much better than this.

And that was what made it so bittersweet. It couldn't last because she wasn't his to hold. He didn't have the right to revel in that soft look, to allow himself to look forward to seeing it every morning for the rest of his life.

He was about to extinguish that light in her eyes, and for the life of him, he didn't know how to say what needed to be said.

Her smile was gentle, a little shy…and solely for him.

"Hi," she said.

"Hi, yourself."

"The puppies are growing like weeds," she said in a rush. "I can't believe how frisky they're getting."

It was obvious she wasn't practiced in morning-after etiquette. Sweetly embarrassed, a little unsure. Color heightened in her cheeks with the tender intensity of a rose petal. If he hadn't been in love with her before, he would have fallen right then and there. "Did they wake you?"

"Yes. But I don't mind. Annie's gaining her strength back, too."

"That's because she's had such a good nurse-maid."

"Plural." She rose with the puppy in her arms, her smile soft. "You've spent more time with them than I have."

He waited until she put Pal back in the cardboard enclosure before he spoke again.

"I got a call from Mr. B."

She turned, her eyes filling with worry. He hated to see that flicker of fear that chased the color from her face. This woman should have only happiness in her life. She shouldn't have to fret about kidnapping attempts or bank loans or the expectations of society. She should have the world at her feet and nothing but time on her hands to devote to her beloved horses.

Tanner knew he could give part of that to her—the money and the time. He just wasn't sure about the expectations of society. *His* presence would more than likely disrupt her life.

He wanted to think it wouldn't. He wanted to believe she'd return home and break her engagement to Latrobe, to admit that there could only be one man for her. Him.

But that scenario gave him a little trouble. Once given, Jordan's word was gold. He admired that about her—hell, he even tried to put himself in Latrobe's place, imagining the devastation the other man would suffer if Jordan dumped him.

He told himself not to dwell on it. Because after last night... And looking at her now, he wasn't in the mood to play fair.

"Well?" she prompted. "Are you going to tell me what Mr. B. said?"

It seemed he was always getting sidetracked around this woman. "Sonny's sounded the all clear. It's safe for you to go home." *I hope.*

"But what about the kidnappers?"

"Evidently they were just a couple of goons out for a quick buck." He deliberately focused his gaze on Annie who was keeping a close eye on her frolicking offspring. He didn't want Jordan to detect the vital information he was leaving out. "They won't be a problem."

"How do you know?"

"Because Sonny spoke to them."

"*Spoke* to them?"

He imagined Sonny had done quite a bit more than that, but wasn't about to speculate on details. Especially with Jordan. "You don't want to know any more."

"Handy friends you have, Caldwell. I still don't understand why those men chose me, how they knew about my wedding or that my family had money."

"Either dumb luck or the fact that the details of your upcoming wedding were splashed in every big-city newspaper around." He shrugged. "That's how I found out."

"Oh."

Her smile was strained. He knew it was about to become more so. Stepping closer, he lifted her hands, and held on. "There's more." As gently as possible, he said, "Your father's not well."

She sucked in a breath and paled. Emotion made her eyes go liquid. "What's wrong with him? What happened?"

"They think it's a heart attack. He's in the hospital."

"Oh, no. I've got to talk to him!" Her voice rose in panic. She jerked away and raced for the bedroom. He followed, and found her tearing through his duffel, scattering clothes at will. "Where is that damned telephone? You tell me the code right now!"

"Easy, Blackie." He reached for her, to soothe,

but she shrugged away. Defiance spit like licks of fire from her eyes as she drew in a breath, gathering her control like a cloak. It was an amazing thing to watch, that core of steel that turned her momentary panic into determined acceptance.

She hadn't fallen apart when strangers had attempted to abduct her, nor when he'd whisked her away from her comfort zone into uncertainty. She'd adapted, made the best of it, kept her spirit.

She was doing the same now. And he admired the hell out of her.

"I intend to call the hospital and let my father know that I'm on my way home."

Tanner nodded and picked up the cell phone from the mattress where he'd left it. "I know." He punched in the code, handed the receiver to her. "I'll be ready to go when you are. Just dial Information and tell them the name of the hospital. The service will automatically connect you."

Her features softened in gratitude as she followed his instructions.

He left the room to give her some privacy, using the time to lock up and formulate a plan for the dogs, who needed care. To his surprise, Pal and Buddy were sprawled close to Annie, nursing.

"Good job, Annie," he murmured, relieved and incredibly touched by the sight. He'd had a hand in bringing this family together, in giving them a chance.

Now he was about to reunite another family. Jordan's. But that thought stirred up a host of emotions that had nothing to do with relief.

As he watched, Annie nudged her babies, then turned proud brown eyes up to Tanner. "Looks like you can handle the fort for a few hours while I'm gone.'' Knowing Jordan would want as few delays as possible, he made sure there was water and food for Annie and spread fresh newspapers on the floor. He doubted he'd be gone long anyway.

If there was no danger to Jordan, he wouldn't be needed anymore. She had a life to live. And even after what they'd shared, he wasn't sure where, or *if* he fitted into that life.

''I'm ready to go.''

He turned, surprised he hadn't heard her come into the room. His self-preservation instincts were getting rusty. Either that, or the weight of despair over losing her was cloaking them.

''Did they let you talk to him?''

''He's already left the hospital,'' she said. ''I tried calling my mother, but evidently she's on her way home from picking Daddy up.''

''Was it a heart attack?''

She shrugged. ''They don't know. Bess, our housekeeper, said the doctors seem to think his symptoms were brought on by stress. He's been instructed to schedule himself in for tests to be sure, but Daddy was adamant about going home. He refused to be stuck in a hospital while I'm still missing.''

She closed her eyes against the guilt, tugged at the hem of her sleeveless denim shirt. ''I should have kept in touch. Told him not to worry.'' She opened her eyes, stared at him. ''Why couldn't I have done that, Tanner?''

Her tone held accusation. She was looking to lay blame, and it was fairly evident that she'd chosen herself as the target.

Tanner wanted to ease that. He was used to shouldering blame. And he wouldn't make matters worse by telling her what they suspected—that Maynard Grazer had been *in* on the abduction. Or behind it, at least. A plan that had gone awry and out of Grazer's control.

"If I had it to do over again, I still wouldn't have wanted you making scheduled phone calls. I made the decisions I thought best for your safety, Jordan."

"Yes, and look what happened. Daddy worked himself into a near heart attack. He's had losing the estate on his mind, the wedding, and then the worry over me being gone. I should have overruled your decision and kept in touch with him."

But if she had, they wouldn't have made love, they wouldn't have gotten to know each other on neutral ground, learned how much they had in common…how right they were for each other.

He wouldn't have had the opportunity to touch, to taste, to store the memory.

It made Tanner wonder if, in a way, he hadn't been worse than the would-be kidnappers. Oh, he'd kept her out of harm's way, but had his reasons been noble or selfish?

"No sense beating yourself up with what-ifs," he said, as much for his own benefit as for hers. "If we leave now, I'll have you back home before your father even has a chance to get settled in bed."

"Thank you." She stepped past him. "What about Annie and the puppies? We can't leave them— Oh, Tanner, look. They're nursing.

"Yeah. Annie seems pleased. I think they'll be just fine on their own until I get back."

She turned then, her gaze meeting his. What

passed between them was so strong it was a wonder the air didn't spark with electricity. There was desire, and sadness and understanding.

Understanding that reality had intruded and time had run out.

Damn it, it seemed that time was always running out for him where Jordan Grazer was concerned. His jaw tight, emotions roiling, he whirled and checked the lock on the kitchen window.

"I figured I'd keep the dogs here for now. You'll have enough on your plate, dealing with your father's health. I've still got some time on my hands, so I'll baby-sit the runts."

The locks were as secure as they were going to get, and he could tell she was antsy to get going. For that matter, so was he—antsy for action, for closure, to know if he had a chance with her or if this trip to town would really be the end.

His head knew the answer; his heart held out hope.

"Do you have everything?"

She held her hands out from her sides. "I came with only the clothes on my back. Other than the shoes that I pitched in the trash, there's nothing to leave behind."

Just the lingering of her scent and the vivid memories, he thought.

And the shattered pieces of his heart.

"Fine, then. Let's go." As he ushered her out the door, he started to scrape his hair back into a ponytail—something he was accustomed to doing in the business world.

That "Take me as I am" voice echoed inside him, staying his hands. He told himself he wasn't putting

Jordan to any tests—he was simply defying Maynard, daring the man to form additional wrong opinions.

Letting his hair hang free and wild, he helped her onto the Harley, rather than taking the Jeep. It was another petty defiance, but it was damned empowering.

Wouldn't it be a kicker when good old Grazer found out that Tanner Caldwell could buy him ten times over?

That little secret would wait for a while, though. He wanted to be looking his old enemy in the eye when he told him.

Perversely, he wanted to gloat. He had an idea it would be the only satisfaction he could call upon, once Jordan was ensconced back in the bosom of her family and her life.

And back in the arms of her fiancé.

Chapter Eleven

Jordan felt like a mother hen counting her chicks as the motorcycle roared up the long driveway leading to the ranch house. A wonderful sense of the familiar settled over her like the comfort of a favorite blanket—the smells, the sights. Horses cropped in grassy fields, and a busy-tailed squirrel scampered up an arching valley oak. Golden buttercups spread out like a mat of welcoming happy faces along the borders of the concrete drive.

The relief she felt over everything appearing the same was so all-encompassing, she nearly shouted out her joy.

The low-throated, bestial sound of the Harley had animals and field hands alike raising heads, looking for the source of disturbance. Honor Bleu whinnied and trotted over to the fence rail as though intending to match his power against the machine's. She grinned when he snorted and pawed at the ground, then trotted the perimeter of the fence, tracking them, his fiercely competitive spirit urging him to pour on the speed more than he should have dared within the confines of the pasture.

Tanner seemed to notice the competition, and

slowed the bike. Silky mane shifting in the wind, black coat shining like indigo velvet against the bright sunlight, Bleu lengthened his stride, muscles bunching, hooves digging in and throwing clumps of loamy sod.

"Is that beauty racing us?" he shouted over his shoulder.

Jordan tightened her arms around his waist, leaning closer to his ear. "Makes you want to start rooting, doesn't it? He never could stand for anyone to be in front of him. That's what made him such a winner. His arrogance can make him a handful sometimes."

Tanner nodded and Jordan appreciated the admiration that clearly showed in his features and in the slight curve of his lips as he watched her magnificent stallion. She couldn't remember Randall ever slowing down to enjoy the sight of her Thoroughbred.

The renegade thought dashed her joy and sent her heart pumping in a silent scream.

They were at the doorstep of reality. Literally.

And suddenly, Jordan wanted to turn and run. But to where? And to whom?

Before she could examine those emotions too closely, Tanner was easing off the throttle, then steadying the bike with a booted foot as he came to a stop beneath the portico. The front door opened almost immediately.

Jordan barely had a chance to swing herself off the motorcycle before the housekeeper was snatching her into a hug.

"Oh, sweet darlin'!" Bess cried. "We've been so worried. I nearly had to sit on your papa when I told him you'd called. Hasn't given me a moment's peace since he came through the door. Had me repeat every word you'd said. Here they are now. He'll be a world better just to touch you.''

"Jordan!" Lydia Grazer rushed out, her arms replacing Bess's. "Are you okay, honey? Are you injured? We've not eaten or slept since this whole, horrible mix-up."

Jordan frowned, her attention on her father, who sat silently in a wheelchair at the open doorway. He looked old and frail—something she'd never before associated with her daddy. Dragging her gaze away for the moment, she asked, "What 'mix-up,' Mother?"

Lydia frowned as though she was convinced Jordan had misplaced her good sense. "The wedding, darling...and you being taken away on that—that motorcycle."

Jordan glanced at Tanner. Dark sunglasses hid his eyes, masking his emotions. His body language spoke volumes, though. Slouched on the bike like a cocky hoodlum, he didn't intend to cut anybody any slack. He obviously expected the worst from her family and had decided to act accordingly.

But Jordan knew him, had touched and looked upon every inch of that body. She knew his heart...and his vulnerabilities that bordered on shame over the cards that had been dealt him at birth.

As she stood beneath the portico, she felt torn. In the doorway sat her father, who was in poor health, whom she hadn't seen in well over a week. Yet, on the other side of her was Tanner, proud and aloof and unsure of his welcome. She didn't know which of them to go to, which one needed her more.

The almost-imperceptible shake of Tanner's head made up her mind. He didn't need or want his hand held. Her father, however, did need the attention.

Strain showed in the lines of Maynard's rounded face. He wore a bathrobe and slippers, which told her just how poorly he was feeling. Maynard Grazer was finicky about his appearance.

To him, it was a measure of acceptance, and anything less than perfect was unacceptable.

She knelt beside the wheelchair and leaned into his open arms. Steel-gray whiskers snagged in her hair and the pulse at his neck beat faster than she would have liked.

"I'm sorry, Daddy."

His green eyes were liquid with emotion that he rarely allowed. "Nothing for you to be sorry about, sweet pea. I've been worried damn near into my grave."

"I know. And that's what I'm apologizing for. All things considered, we thought it would be best to keep a low profile until things blew over." She fussed with his robe, worried over the florid hue of his cheeks. "But let's not talk about that now. I'm safe...thanks to Tanner."

"Caldwell?" He said the name as though it stank to high heaven. "I knew there was something familiar about him. You go on in the house, now. We'll call the sheriff."

Jordan sucked in a breath. "Daddy! No, you misunderstood. Tanner saved me from being kidnapped. Didn't you see the van follow us out of town? I explained—"

"You didn't explain diddly. For all I knew, some madman had a gun to your head making you say those words."

"No. No madman. But if someone had gone to the trouble of trying to take me right from my wedding, they could have easily tapped your telephones. Until Sonny knew—"

"Sonny?"

Jordan sighed, feeling as though she'd walked into the middle of a play where the entire cast didn't have a clue about the plot or their next lines. "Sonny works with Tanner."

"You mean that son of a B *lied* to me?"

"Daddy, this is a long story and we don't need to get into it on the front porch. Besides, you need to be resting. Let's get you back inside." She gripped the handles of the wheelchair, and glanced at Tanner.

He inclined his head and gave her a silent salute. A farewell.

Her stomach felt lodged in her throat. *Don't go,* she wanted to plead. But she knew he wouldn't push his presence on her father—not when Maynard was in poor health. He wouldn't approach without an invitation.

But Maynard wouldn't even acknowledge Tanner's presence; the few feet of distance between them might well have been a chasm the size of the Grand Canyon. The solid, equal ground she and Tanner had shared for one and a half glorious weeks had shifted.

Not on her part—never on her part. But her family hadn't changed a bit. Lydia and Bess flanked her;

Maynard sat front and center, looking weak, yet still the lord of the manner.

And Tanner sat alone. Always so alone.

"We owe him a lot, Daddy," she said quietly, her throat raw with the ache of repressed emotions. "A thank-you at the very least. He kept me safe and saved us a loss of money. There was a ransom note."

"So you said. Who's to say he didn't write it himself?"

Shock and anger stole her breath. "Oh, the two of you are so much alike it's scary!" When Tanner had accused her father, he'd claimed he'd just been grabbing at straws. Now she had to wonder if it wasn't pure rivalry between these two stubborn men.

"What's that supposed to mean?" Maynard demanded.

"Never mind." Feeling embarrassed by her father's lack of gratitude toward Tanner, she forced a smile and called softly, "Thank you, Tanner. Will you stay for lunch?"

Even from this distance she saw the twin dimples that crept slowly into his cheeks. The thrill that shot through her was swift and incendiary. And terribly inappropriate, flanked as she was by her family.

But, oh, he was so...so *male*. With him, she could be a little wild, a little carefree. And a whole lot feminine.

"Maybe another time, Blackie. But thank you kindly for the offer of hospitality."

"Blackie?" Maynard echoed in disapproval. The address was leveled at Jordan, and if he'd picked up on Tanner's subtle sarcasm, he didn't give any indication. Before she could think of an appropriate platitude, a pricey sedan came barreling down the lane.

Her spirits hit rock bottom. "Did someone call Randall?"

"Damn straight, somebody did," Maynard said. "I did. Have you already forgotten that you were supposed to be married to him by now?"

Not forgotten entirely. Just dismissed. Like Scarlett O'Hara, she'd vowed to think about it tomorrow.

Well, tomorrow had just arrived, driving a champagne-colored Mercedes-Benz.

And although Randall didn't normally go in for public displays of affection, she decided not to take a chance. Right now, she couldn't think of anything more uncomfortable than being swept into the arms of another man in front of Tanner.

Even if that other man was her intended husband.

Releasing the wheelchair brake with a jerk, she quickly backed Maynard over the front-door threshold.

JORDAN PLEADED exhaustion, and it worked on Randall. She'd answered as many questions as she could—not that *she* had all the answers she wanted. The whole affair still puzzled her, made her edgy.

Randall hadn't insisted on hanging around or hand-holding, even though he'd only been there for a half hour. Although he wasn't one to fuss or get mushy and maudlin—a trait she'd appreciated about him—he could have at least shown a little more concern; jealousy, at the very least, over the fact that she'd spent time—*alone*—with another man. But he'd simply dismissed all that, kissed her lightly on the cheek and said that it had all worked out for the best, and now that she was home safe and sound, the town's name wouldn't be dragged through the mud in nasty headlines.

Piqued, Jordan figured she ought to have rated at least a little higher than the price of real estate in the eyes of her fiancé.

Now, with Randall headed home and her father forced into bed rest—a combined effort of nagging from the Grazer women—Jordan was chomping at the bit to check on her horses.

And to meet the famous Mr. B.

Frankly, Jordan thought as she made her way out to the stables, she'd been mortified to learn that her father had assigned the man Sonny's room in the bunkhouse.

Millionaire Samuel Bartholomew in the *bunkhouse,* for pete's sake!

Daddy must have assumed Mr. B. was merely a hired hand—sometimes her father's judgment of folks was seriously flawed. She'd always known he was crusty and arrogant. He had a good heart, though. Even if he didn't show that side of himself to others very often, Jordan knew it was there.

Grabbing a lead rope someone had left hanging on the fence post, Jordan entered the corral and whistled softly to Bleu. He trotted over, snorting and tossing his head, hanging back a few feet as though to punish her for having left him in the hands of strangers.

"Come on over here," she chided, yet closed the distance herself. Sometimes she could swear the stallion had human thoughts. Arrogant, *male* human thoughts. "Pretend all you want, champ. You know darn well you'll always love me." She slipped the rope around Bleu's powerful neck. "Besides, didn't I leave you in good hands? Tanner claims Sonny's the best." She gave the horse a kiss on the nose—a gesture not many could get away with. Bleu could get ornery, and liked to bite. He'd nipped her a time or two in the early days, the days before they'd bonded.

Now she trusted him completely. He would never intentionally harm her. Maybe step on her foot a time or two, but that was her own fault for not staying out of the way.

As they neared the cool, shadowy interior of the stables, Jordan's heart lurched. Tanner's Harley was parked off to the side.

So, he hadn't left, after all. She was happier about that than she should have been. Especially since her fiancé had just driven off, fully under the impression that everything about their relationship was still status quo.

And wasn't it?

The loan was still pending; no one had spoken about promises being broken. After explanations had been handed out all around, the attitudes in the Grazer household were the same. She'd been granted time to settle, then the wedding plans would be resurrected.

Curiously, her mother was the only one—besides Jordan herself—who'd been less than enthusiastic, graciously changing the subject when it had arisen, so subtly that no one had noticed.

Except Jordan.

Maybe there was an ally there, in her mother.

Bleu butted her with his nose as though he'd read

her thoughts and was determined to remind her of her place.

And it worked. Oh, what was she thinking? She had no business lining up allies. She had obligations to uphold.

"Don't worry, Bleu," she murmured. "We won't lose the ranch or the stables." Her hand tightened around the lead rope. "I won't lose you." The weight on her shoulders felt like a ton.

Tanner had his back to her when she led Bleu into the wide aisle of the barn where stalls flanked both sides. Horses snorted greetings and munched on hay, most with their beautiful heads hanging over the stall gates.

The man deep in conversation with Tanner lifted his head and gave a beaming smile. Dark hair shot liberally with gray was combed straight back from a face lined with plenty of character. He was a tall man, his body in good shape, though she estimated his age somewhere in the mid- to late-sixties. Probably a home gym, state-of-the-art, she figured. If this was Tanner's Mr. B., he could afford the best.

He didn't look like a millionaire. She wasn't sure what she'd expected. A suit? Fingers dripping in gold? A Rolex winking beneath a starched cuff?

Instead, he wore a simple polo shirt in cotton-candy pink, gray slacks and high-top sneakers.

"Jordan Grazer, I presume?" he asked, smiling, stepping up to her. As gallant as you please, he lifted her free hand and kissed her knuckles.

Jordan was charmed right down to her boots. And amused. The Rolex she'd expected was actually a whimsical wristwatch sporting a Tasmanian Devil.

Grinning, she sketched a slight curtsy. "And you'd be Mr. B.?"

"Ah, Samuel to you, surely."

"Samuel, it is."

Tanner stepped up beside his friend. For a second she thought he was going to reach for her. Instead, he extended his hand to Bleu.

"Careful," Jordan warned. "He's been known to bite."

"Mmm. And I've been known to bite back."

Jordan felt her face flame. He wasn't talking about horses. And oh, the remembrance of his brand of biting was so powerful, so thrilling, she was sure her thoughts showed on her face.

She spared a quick glance at Samuel. The man winked and her face grew even hotter.

Holding Bleu steady, she waited to see how beast and man would size each other up. Bleu jerked his head, pulling against the lead rope, his nostrils wide. Eerie eyes that appeared more human than animal took Tanner's measure.

In tune to Bleu's every nuance, she felt him settle, watched in amazement as he turned into a pussycat right before her eyes. If the stallion could have purred, he'd have done so as Tanner stroked his neck, between his eyes and down to his nose, giving him plenty of opportunity to register his scent.

And why wouldn't he purr? Jordan thought. Tanner's touch had that effect.

And it thrilled her to see these two males who both meant so much to her, becoming friends.

"Fine piece of horseflesh," Mr. B. commented. "You interested in selling?"

Jordan's hand jerked on the rope, startling the

stallion. He did a sidestep shuffle, then swung his massive head around in what appeared to be accusation.

"Sorry, boy. Easy, now." Patting the horse's neck, she unconsciously took a step closer to his side. To Samuel, she said, "Never."

"Sure? I'll offer a damn good price. Honor Bleu would make a fine addition to my stables."

"Positive. No amount of money could get me to part with this horse."

"Can't blame a man for trying."

"No. You have excellent taste."

Tanner watched as she settled her horse in his stall. The love she had for the animal was so evident. Swiftly, and irrationally, he felt jealous of a horse. What would it be like to have someone so devoted to him? To have someone care so deeply?

Once she was finished with her task, she came out of the stall, checked the latch, then wiped her palms on her jeans and turned toward him.

He thought he might drown in those green eyes. There was longing there, but there was also worry. His protective instincts rose. Then he realized that worry was for him.

He tried to turn away from it, didn't want it, but she spoke before he could find a civil way to excuse himself.

"I'm sorry for the way my family treated you, Tanner."

He shrugged. "No big deal." The shame of non-acceptance was still there, but not as strong as it might have been. This time, when confronted by Grazer's snub, Tanner wasn't alone. He'd had Mr. B. to give him balance, to remind him that there was someone who cared. To remind him that he wasn't that poor-white-trash kid who'd left town all those years ago.

And one of the things he appreciated about Samuel, was that he didn't butt in indiscriminately—he understood about a man's pride. What he did do was simply provide strength through his quiet presence alone.

Jordan, however, didn't appear to think about pride, and she had no compunction about jumping in and defending.

"It *is* a big deal," she insisted. "You saved Daddy a lot of money in ransom. You might even have saved my life. My family owes you gratitude and hospitality, not a cold shoulder."

"Don't sweat it, Blackie. I'm a big boy and I can handle it when somebody doesn't want to share the toys or play with me."

He heard what could only be described as a growl deep in her throat. She was working up a head of steam—on his behalf.

He nearly grinned but thought better of it.

Samuel, however, wasn't as smart. The man threw back his head and gave a booming laugh. Jordan's head whipped around, and Tanner had enough sense to take a discreet step back.

"Do share the amusement, Mr. Bartholomew."

"Ah, the deb's back," Tanner murmured.

"Shut up, Tanner." But she smiled through the words, still waiting for Mr. B. to explain his hyena imitation.

"For a minute there, you reminded me of someone I met in town."

"Who?"

"Agatha Flintstone. A fine woman, that. Owns the Book Nook."

"Agatha?" Jordan said weakly, clearly astonished. "'A fine woman'?"

"Absolutely. You know her, my dear?"

"Well, yes." She glanced at Tanner as if to question the sanity of his friend.

"The woman's got spunk. Claimed you'd been hauled off on a snorting beast of a motorcycle and how it was terribly romantic. Just like a Norman conqueror of old."

"Uh…yes, she does tend to think in terms of her romance novels."

"And that's another thing," Samuel said. "A woman who reads romance shows excellent sense and taste. I read 'em myself. Gives a man plenty of good advice…and some wonderful guidance. Why, I just might give some thought to that Norman-conqueror thing."

Tanner nearly strangled on a swallow. His head whipped around so fast his own untied hair slapped him in the face. Good God, if he wasn't mistaken—and he doubted seriously that he was—Mr. B. had just subtly stated his intention to fulfil Agatha Flintstone's wildest fantasy.

Noticing that Jordan, too, was making a womanly effort to keep her jaw from dropping, he stepped into the breach. "I think this is a good time to make a dignified exit."

Mr. B. sniffed. "There's not one undignified thing about what I said. Those of us in our golden years are entitled to have fun, too, you know." His brows drew together—as though he'd forgotten something vital—then shot upward. "Oh, I do beg your pardon,

Miss Jordan. I see now that my friend is gently trying to remind me that I might have offended your sensibilities. I'm a romantic old fool, and I have a tendency to forget myself at times. Please accept my apology.''

Looking thoroughly charmed now, Jordan reached out and gave Samuel's arm a squeeze. "No need to apologize. I assure you, my sensibilities are fairly unshakable. And you are absolutely right, Samuel. Romance is timeless. I, for one, will be rooting for you." She cleared her throat, sounding suspiciously like she was strangling a chuckle. "And for Agatha, of course."

"Thank you, my dear."

Now Tanner definitely knew it was time to leave. Her green eyes were shining, her soft lips stretched into a smile. She made him ache just to look at her; made him want. And being so close to Jordan and unable to touch her, to take her to bed, to spend time with her, was pure torture.

"The two of you look like you can handle things from here," Tanner said. "I'll catch you later."

The happy smile left Jordan's face. "You're leaving?"

"I need to check on the dogs."

"But—"

He couldn't help himself. He had to touch her, With a single finger, he caressed her lips. stopping her words. Wanting to linger, knowing he'd never have the strength to leave if he did, he pulled back and stuffed his hands in his pockets.

"Mr. B. will be here if you need anything." Left

unspoken was the fact that Samuel would be welcome to stay on Grazer property. Tanner would not.

"You need time to get reacquainted with your family," he said softly. "If you need me, Mr. B. can find me."

Chapter Twelve

Tanner headed the Jeep toward Grazer's Vineyards. He'd given Jordan two days to settle in, using the time to do his own subtle investigation, talking with the people in town, checking the buzz. Small towns were notorious for gossip. He was a little surprised by the curiosity and acceptance this town extended him. Expecting to be met with censure, prepared to either field or ignore questions about his father, he hadn't exactly behaved in a charming manner.

The hell of it was, nobody seemed to notice. They treated him like a returning hero because he'd saved their golden girl.

The endless questions and speculations about Mr. B. tipped him off. He had an idea his friend had gone before him, singing his praises to anyone who would listen. Agatha Flintstone was at the head of the fan club.

Well, that would probably change soon enough. Once Maynard Grazer was back on his feet, he wouldn't waste any time reminding the good folks of Grazer's Corners who Tanner really was, who his father had been. The old adage Breeding Will Tell flashed through his mind.

He'd thought he didn't care anymore. But he did. Not just for himself, but for how it would affect Jordan.

With the whole town aware and alert for potential danger, Tanner figured it would take an armored tank to get past the lines and to Jordan if someone was stupid enough to make another attempt.

Driving around to the back of the stables, he stopped the Jeep, then opened the rear door. "Let's go, girl," he called to Annie, lifting the box he'd put Buddy and Pal in. The puppies scrambled up, tripped over each other and scratched at the sides of the box.

He grinned at their antics. He'd miss these little guys.

The interior of the stables was cool and smelled of animals and hay and grain, of liniment and leather. Horses hung their heads over chest-high doors, whickering softly to one another. A concrete aisleway, sloped for drainage, ran through the center of the open ended structure.

He found Jordan in Honor Bleu's stall with her arms around the stallion, cheek to cheek as though they were sharing intimate secrets—or saying good-bye. Something shifted inside him, a fierce protectiveness. Jordan Grazer shouldn't have so many responsibilities on her shoulders. He wanted to ease her burdens but was afraid that in trying to do so, he might just add to them.

Money could buy peace of mind, pay off mortgages and update supplies, but it couldn't buy acceptance.

And in her family's eyes, Tanner was far from acceptable.

He stood where he was for another moment, drinking in the sight of woman and horse. Both had glossy midnight hair, hair so black it nearly shone blue. It was hard to tell where one left off and the other began. And what a sight they made, both of them sleek and beautiful...so unique.

The stallion reared his head and Jordan whirled.

"Oh, you startled me." Soon enough, though, fear vanished, and her green eyes lit with welcome, making him feel as though he'd come home at last.

Was there hope? he wondered. Could he belong here? In her life? Dear God, he was afraid to let that yearning take hold, afraid that she was a star, and that his reach would only extend as far as the moon.

"I brought you something," he said quietly.

"So I see." She closed the door to Bleu's stall, then bent down to pat Annie before treating each of the puppies to a playful tickle. "I thought you were going to keep them."

"They'll be happier out here."

She gave him a long, searching look, a look that held sadness and understanding. She knew he was here to tell her goodbye. He turned away.

"You just missed Samuel." She stood, leaving the puppies to play in their box.

"I know. I called him and told him I was coming."

"Are the two of you taking shifts with me?" She patted the cheek of a chestnut yearling who occupied the stall opposite Bleu's. "Do you suspect another attempt?"

"No. I'm fairly certain you're safe. As for Mr. B., I'm having a hard time dragging him away from your horses."

Jordan smiled even though her heart wasn't in it. She understood the significance of him bringing the puppies. He would be hitting the road soon, a maverick on a Harley who had yet to find his roots, a place he wanted to stay long enough to allow pets.

"Samuel appreciates fine stock. It's hard not to fall in love with them." She noticed how Tanner automatically reached out to stroke Bleu, and her pulse leaped at the sight of those beautiful, scarred hands stroking her horse. Images of those hands on *her* were keeping her up at night.

Afraid she'd cry...or beg, she forced a smile. "I swear Bleu's turning into an old woman right before my eyes. He rarely lets people get this close—especially men. Now he's taken a shine to three of you—Sonny, Samuel and you."

"Shows he's got good taste. And shame on you for calling him an old woman. It's plain as day he's all male."

"True." They were like wary opponents, circling, each reluctant to make the first move. And oh, how she wanted to take that initial step. She wanted to kiss him, to ease into his arms and lose herself in passion. He had his hair tied into a ponytail today, wore threadbare Levi's and a T-shirt that fit him like a second skin. The epitome of a bad boy. Yet the gentle way he stroked Bleu was at odds with his clenched-jaw look, and it was creating all sorts of fantasies.

"So why is it that Bleu's leery around men?"

"I don't know, since I never actually met the previous owners." She noticed that he kept looking at her as if measuring the distance between them, as if contemplating the feasibility of using the hay in one of the stalls as a bed. It made her palms sweat.

"Of course, the way he's taken to you and your friends, maybe it's just the men around here he doesn't like. Then again, perhaps you've just got the right touch." He certainly did with her. "Even injured, he was a handful for the vets at UC Davis."

"Is that where you got him?"

She nodded. "We heard about him through a friend of Daddy's and drove out to Davis to have a look. He was a Kentucky Derby winner with impeccable lineage, but on his last race, a freak accident caused hairline cracks in his leg. He was healing and the vets couldn't keep him much longer, but the owner didn't seem to want him back. He'd just dropped him off like a used towel. One look into those spirited eyes and I had to have him."

"Even if he was washed up on the racing circuit, didn't the owner see the potential as breeding stock?"

"No. Very few did, for that matter. Bleu's got spirit and style and stamina, but he's also got a mean streak that comes across as unmanageability. He could be considered a wild card, chancy." She picked up a currycomb that had fallen off the ledge and set it aside. "I didn't agree. I believe that those qualities are what gave him the drive and determination to win—I told you he's stubborn and hates for another horse to get in front of him. He's the type of horse that if he wants to go left and you want to go right, you go left. He wants things his way."

"A little like his owner, hmm? Bet the two of you have gone a few rounds."

"A few. Some of them, he even lets me win."

She glanced fondly at the stallion. "That's because he has heart. I knew that right away, the first time I laid eyes on him, and that's what makes him special. Ask anything of him and he'll give it. Right off, I'd have laid money that he'd produce winners. All I needed was the right mare who wouldn't cost me an arm and a leg."

"Find her?"

"Yeah. I pored over the circuit news, watching for retired or injured horses. That's how I got Pride of Chance. She was languishing on a ranch out in San Jacinto. Most people are really good to their horses—then there are others who ought to be shot for their shoddy treatment and lack of caring."

He reached out and plucked a piece of straw from her hair. "So you rescue strays and champion the underdog."

Something in his voice made her pause. He might as well have added, "Like me." It was there in the barest flicker of his whiskey eyes. *Yes,* she almost responded. *And I fall in love with all of them—like you.*

But she wasn't free to voice that thought, to feel that emotion. And that made her eyes sting. Since her palms were itching to touch, she curled them into fists.

"I don't see it as rescuing strays. I simply look past the obvious and determine the potential."

"And if you found one who didn't have potential?"

For some reason, she thought he was asking a deeper question, one that had nothing to do with livestock. In any case, she answered honestly. "I'd still bring them home. There's plenty of interest in good riding stock.''

''For your handicapped kids?''

''How did you know about them?''

''Heard about it in town. Agatha Flintstone appears to know quite a bit about your life. She admires you.''

Jordan grinned, regaining her balance. ''You've been talking to Agatha?''

''Figured I'd screen her for Mr. B., especially since he's building kinky fantasies around the woman.''

She laughed then, feeling lighter somehow. ''What do you think?''

''Well, you're right. I could imagine stuff more kinky than—''

She swatted him on the arm. ''Not about the fantasy. About Agatha.''

''Strange, eccentric, no-nonsense. Has her finger on the pulse of the town. Smart, with a real sweet streak running through her that most folks don't recognize.''

''You're very astute.''

''And you're a softie. If you're going to breed winners, Blackie, you have to let go. You can't fall in love with each one, tame them, keep them.''

Just like she couldn't tame or keep Tanner. ''Are we talking about horses?''

A tightening at the corners of his eyes gave him away. ''What else?''

She decided to let it pass. ''Whether I fall in love with them or not doesn't change the fact that I've got a good start. Bleu will sire winners. He might be a little hard to handle, rough around the edges, but he's still a gentleman.''

"Leaves his lady well satisfied?''

Just that quickly, desire shot through her. It was the look in his eyes, the devilish spark that vied with the heat. And oh, how she knew *he* would leave his lady satisfied.

But she wasn't his lady.

That didn't keep her from wanting him, though; from wanting to ignore the obligations of her world for just a little longer.

She looked away, afraid that if she didn't, she'd do something highly inappropriate.

And get away with it, she realized. They were alone. The opportunity was there. Her heart pounded harder. She had to stop her thoughts from straying to the possibilities of her and Tanner as a couple—in bed.

To distract herself, she lifted the puppies out of their box and headed toward the tack room that led to the bunkhouse. With a practiced eye, she noted each glossy chestnut yearling and filly she passed, making a mental note to get the latch repaired on Serendipity's stall.

To an outsider, the stables would appear to be in tip-top condition, but Jordan saw beyond the tidy white walls and freshly washed concrete. It took money to keep this place up.

The weight of responsibility settled over her again. She loved the smell of the stables, the familiar feel. She couldn't lose it, couldn't do that to Daddy or to her horses.

For her family, for the precious lives of her animals, she had to go through with the marriage to Randall.

She heard Tanner's footsteps in her wake, and a horrible ache welled inside her.

Maynard still needed the loan from Randall's bank, and the added medical expense that had just cropped up made their situation so much worse.

Granted, their sketchy finances were due in part to Maynard not wanting to lower his standard of living. But she'd benefited from those standards, had accepted the cars and credit cards and horses, hadn't questioned the source of the funds that kept the stables running.

Until it was almost too late.

She *owed* her father. And as much as she wanted to take something for herself, to beg Tanner to stay—or to take her with him when he left—she couldn't.

They'd both known the score, known that she wasn't free to build a future with him. Still, it didn't make the idea of parting any easier to accept.

Leather slapped against the wall as Tanner fiddled with the tack. "So, how's it going with Russell?"

She nearly bobbled the puppies. "Randall," she muttered automatically, wondering if he'd somehow tapped into her thoughts. But she didn't want to think about Randall now. Not with Tanner standing so close. "Things are fine."

"Funny, you still don't look like an eager bride."

She caught a whiff of his scent, clean and masculine. Her nerves jumped like a skittish filly's. "You've been around a lot of brides, have you?"

"Just the one I stole off the church steps."

"Rescued," she corrected, unable to look away from the gentleness in his eyes.

He touched her cheek. "You change your mind?"

Her eyes closed on a wave of despair. "I know what's expected of me."

Tanner wanted to shake her. "You'll still go through with it? Even after what we shared up at the lake?"

Her eyes flashed open. "Yes."

His breath hissed. "It's about money again, isn't it?"

"I won't give up my horses." Her shoulders squared. "And I won't give up on Daddy."

"Hell, Jordan, *I'll* make the damned loan."

"How? By asking Samuel?" She didn't give him a chance to answer. She eased up to him, laid a hand on his chest. "I can't let you do that."

He opened his mouth, admission right there, but she placed a fingertip across his lips. An erotic current sparked straight to his brain, then bolted like lightning right to his jeans, making him rigid.

"We both knew, Tanner."

Knew that she was to be married. To another man. A country-club hobnobber with soft hands, perfectly styled blond hair, impeccable manners and a politician's smile.

Tanner felt like smashing his fists into the nearest wall.

"Can't your old man see this isn't what you want?"

She wouldn't hold his gaze.

He tipped a finger under her chin, urged her to look at him. "Maynard's ticked that *I'm* the one who had you." In more ways than one. "The son of a Caldwell."

"I'm sorry," she said softly. "Daddy's set in his ways."

"Have the two of you fought?"

Although he still held her chin, her eyes lowered. An answer in itself.

And that was when Tanner's hope died, when he realized that it wouldn't work. She had the weight of the world—or at least of her family's estate—on her shoulders. His presence only made her burden heavier. If he stayed, if he pushed, he would only cause a rift between Jordan and her family.

And family was important to her.

He couldn't do it. He loved her enough to let her go.

Even as he resigned himself to the heartache, she threw him a curve by gripping his shirtfront and pulling him into a kiss that had the ground shifting beneath his feet.

"I know it's wrong," she said against his lips. "I can't seem to help myself. I want you, Tanner."

Want. Dear God, he knew about wanting. He'd spent a good portion of his life yearning for what other people took for granted. The simple peace of acceptance, to be able to walk down the street without having to use his fists to defend that right.

And as he'd grown, suffered through the hard knocks of life, those wants had shifted, expanded. He'd craved power and respect, and the money that would ensure both.

But even those obsessions paled in comparison to what Jordan made him feel. She stripped his mind clean until there was nothing left but naked sensation.

Her lips were eager and greedy and just a little desperate. He, too, felt that desperation, that need. As razor sharp as a hunting knife, it stripped away the layers of manners and civilized ethics he'd carved out for himself, honed over the years. Everything about this woman, her touch, her scent, drove him mad, unleashed the reckless man beneath the careful exterior.

"Hell, Jordan, let's take this somewhere else. Anybody could walk in."

"No." She jerked his shirttail from the waist of his jeans. "Samuel's gone. Nobody comes out here except Daddy and he's in town at the doctor's." With a frustrated moan, she abandoned his shirt and whipped her own over her head.

Thrown off stride, he felt his mouth fall open. Her shirt went sailing, landing squarely on a saddlehorn that hung from the wall. Her busy fingers worked on the buttons of her jeans and she had them shucked down her legs before he could get his tongue up off the floor.

By damn, she wasn't wearing a stitch under that denim.

"Hold on a second." He kicked the door shut, twisted the lock and yanked his own shirt over his head. "You're getting ahead of me, here. And I'm finding I've got something in common with your horse in that respect."

"Then step up the pace."

"Baby, you're playing with fire."

"No. I'm *on* fire."

"Guess we'd better put it out, then." He consid-

ered leaving his pants on; at the rate they were going, he was likely to lose control in a matter of seconds and embarrass the hell out of himself. But he
pulled them off anyway, not really sure how he managed. His heart was knocking against his chest and
his knees felt like spaghetti.

He stepped up to her, felt his throat go dry as
desert sand at the first touch of skin against skin.
"Just stand there," he said.

"What?" Confusion fairly shouted.

"I want to just kiss you for a while." His voice
thickened, as did the rest of him. "To savor."

Jordan went weak all over as his lips teased and
tasted. Her arms felt weighted at her sides, too heavy
to lift to his shoulders.

"Yeah," he murmured. "Just like that." His lips
cruised over her jaw, feathered over her neck. The
skin of his chest against her breasts sent a hum of
sensation that could well have caused sparks.

"Touch me," she whispered.

"I'll get to it." Eyes open, using only his mouth,
he worshiped her, made love to her from the neck
up. It was a gift, the most powerfully erotic thing
she'd ever experienced.

He cupped a hand at the back of her neck, then
released the clip that held her hair up. Her skin was
so sensitized, she felt each individual strand as it fell
past her shoulders, sweeping a path of chills in its
wake.

She could only stand there, numb, yet so won-
derfully alive.

"I've always loved your hair." He lifted one of
her limp hands and placed it on his shoulder. "Black
as midnight." The other hand now. "I'd see that

color in my sleep, just close my eyes and shut out the world, and there you'd be. All that black hair shining and flowing, bouncing like silk in the wind when you were astride one of your ponies.''

Feeling dizzy, thrilled, needing to hold on, she slid her arms around his neck. "You watched me?"

"Mmm." He toyed with her earlobe, bit down lightly.

Body to body with him now, her skin felt on fire. She pressed against him. "Tanner?"

"Mmm-hmm?" His knuckles skimmed the sides of her breasts.

"I'm not sure how much longer I can breathe."

"Want me to stop?" Even as he said the words his palm was cupping her, his thumb passing erotically over her nipple.

"No. I want you to hurry."

She felt his smile against her lips. "I aim to please."

No, that was her line...her ridiculous motto. And the reminder, even unknowingly couched in eroticism, made her desperation shoot into overdrive. As much as she wanted to savor, to store this memory, her body was demanding more.

So when he backed her up to the desk, it was Jordan who swept the cluttered surface clean with an impatient swipe of her arm. Papers scattered, tack jingled and a bottle of liniment bounced onto the braided oval rug.

He lifted her onto the desk, and bent over her. She tugged his hair loose, hardly aware that her hands were racing over him. Sensations registered through the haze of desire—smooth, sleek muscles bunched and straining, lips branding a trail of fire.

Her lungs burned and she couldn't seem to draw in air fast enough.

With a strength born of runaway emotions, she gripped his hips and pulled him between her legs. Her body tightened like a fist and she could have sworn she saw stars. Light flashed and danced behind her closed lids.

The power of it was too much, the wanting too huge.

"Now, Tanner."

"Wait."

"No. I feel like I'm falling." Her breath heaved in and out. She felt him press against her, so intimately. She wanted him inside her, could barely think past the sensations to coherency. "Catch me."

"I won't let you fall." Tanner eased inside her. "Trust me." Blood pounded in his head like an ancient chant. Although she'd practically begged, he concentrated on using every ounce of control he possessed not to plunge mindlessly into her like an aggressive stallion covering an eager mare.

He wanted it to last, wanted to watch every nuance of her expression, feel every point of pleasure, every flicker of sensation. He needed that; more than he needed air to breathe—needed to imprint the memory.

But her energy and determination outmatched him, sent him straight into a frenzy. He'd have treated her like spun glass if that was what she'd needed at the moment. But she didn't want or need gentleness.

With her legs shackled around his waist, she urged him on, sending him perilously close to oblivion. He reeled with the power of it all, and even as his tempo increased, as his body stood poised on the brink of climax, he mustered that tiny thread of sanity, was able to look down and watch her...

Watch the glory transform her face, the flush that stained her breasts; taste the sweet flavor of surrender on her damp skin. Her muscles squeezed him and her breath hitched in a sob that was his name.

And it took him right over the edge. If nothing else, what they had just shared would ensure one thing—she would always remember his name.

Chapter Thirteen

Aware of the risk of being caught—Maynard could return from the doctor any time now—they dressed in silence.

After what had just taken place in the tiny tack room, she might have been a little embarrassed. Instead, she only felt subdued, as if she'd given a piece of herself away that she'd never recover.

And she had. She'd given her heart and soul.

She bent and retrieved the scattered papers, her gaze straying to Tanner's hands as he buckled his belt. Flies buzzed and horses snorted. The puppies whined and scratched at the box, until Annie poked her nose over the side, soothing them.

And still, she and Tanner spoke no words. The ones she ached to say would not come. *Could* not come.

So she chose different ones, safer ones. "Where will you go now?"

His eyes squinted as though avoiding smoke...or despair. She almost lost her own tenuous hold on control.

He shoved his hands in his pockets. "Back to the

lake, to pick up the bike. Then I'll probably head over to Modesto to check on business.''

She didn't ask him what business. Prolonging their parting would only rip at her heart more. So she simply nodded and walked with him out to the Jeep.

He opened the door, paused. Turning, he laid a palm against her cheek. ''Are you sure, Blackie?''

She knew what he was asking. Was she sure she wanted to marry Randall? Was she sure there was no hope for them?

She'd promised herself she wouldn't cry. The tears betrayed her, slipping down her cheeks. She didn't answer his question. Couldn't answer it. ''Take care of yourself, Tanner,'' she whispered.

For a long moment he just looked at her as though he were memorizing her features. Then he pressed his lips softly to her forehead. ''Likewise, duchess.''

This time when he called her ''duchess,'' there was no derision.

Her heart knocked against her ribs and her hands trembled. As the Jeep's engine fired to life, she stepped back and wrapped her arms around her middle, holding on.

He didn't look back.

A cloud of dust billowed in the wake of the tires. Feeling numb, paralyzed, she watched the taillights disappear down the drive, watched as her love rode away in a borrowed Jeep.

Suddenly she resented everything—her family, the horses, her own dreams.

For a wild instant she considered loading Honor Bleu into the trailer, following Tanner, starting over somewhere else.

Then reality intruded. She couldn't do that to her father. Maynard Grazer had made sacrifices for her. And she was in a position to pay back those sacrifices.

She told herself her heart would mend, promised herself she would not cheat Randall.

She'd be a good wife. The best.

Because when a woman had something to do, had people counting on her, she did what had to be done.

And did it well.

Squaring her shoulders, she went into the house. There was a wedding to salvage, guests to contact. This time, though, they would do it according to her rules. It would be an intimate affair at the church— no fancy country-club reception.

If Randall pitched a fit, *he* could foot the bill for a larger party. No longer were the Grazers going to squander money foolishly—especially to keep up appearances.

Falling in love with Tanner had taught her one very important thing.

Appearances didn't mean squat.

JORDAN RUMMAGED through the drawers of her mother's cherry-wood secretary. Lydia Grazer was a stickler for organization and it showed in the perfectly aligned stationery, and in the individual compartments that held pens by color and pencils by number.

So where the heck was the guest list? The blue-tabbed file marked "Wedding" was empty and though the database of names was computerized, Jordan had been sure there was a hard copy printed out somewhere.

Voices sounded in the hallway. Her parents had returned from the doctor's. She started to call out to her mother, to ask about the list. Then she saw a piece of paper mangled between two drawers. Carefully, she eased the sheet from where it was caught, smoothing out the accordion folds.

Words swam in front of her face and a buzzing sounded in her ears. She dropped into the burgundy leather chair, her fingers trembling.

Ransom.

The word jumped out at her like a stallion rearing at the sight of a snake.

Starting at the beginning, she read each damning word of the letter, her heart sinking, her mind going numb. For several minutes she stared at what appeared to be a discarded note outlining a nefarious scheme—written in her mother's distinctive cursive.

It could have been seconds or hours that she sat like a statue in that chair. The sound of an indrawn breath had her head snapping up, her mind clearing.

Lydia Grazer stood in the doorway, her auburn hair swept into a sophisticated updo style. She looked cool and classy in a sunny yellow suit. Pure silk, Jordan knew. Tasteful, yet expensive.

But Lydia wasn't looking all that cool at the moment. Her green eyes were wide with panic...and guilt.

"Mother," Jordan said.

Lydia drew on her innate composure, walked across the room and took the paper from Jordan's hands. "I should have burned this."

"But you didn't. I'd like an explanation."

"What's to explain?"

Jordan's jaw dropped. "Arranging for the kidnapping of your own daughter isn't call for explanation?''

"It wasn't actually a kidnapping, dear."

So polite. So proper. Jordan nearly screamed. "It certainly looked that way from where *I* was standing. That man...that short, fat one had a gun!"

"Uncle Cyrus?" A frown marred Lydia's chinadoll brow. "I'm sorry, dear. Of course, carrying a weapon was unfortunate and a bit dramatic. I hadn't known."

"A bit?"

"You were never in danger, darling. I can assure you of that. That's why I contacted your Uncle Cyrus and cousin Al in the first place."

Jordan stared at her mother, feeling as though she'd never laid eyes on the woman before.

"Those...those weirdos are my relatives?"

"My aunt's husband and son. Neither has ever amounted to much. We don't socialize."

Little wonder. And though she didn't particularly hold any fondness for the idiots who'd scared her half to death and ruined her wedding day, she also didn't approve of her mother's judgmental attitude. Oh, she'd always been aware of her parents' snobbish view toward less fortunate, less wealthy people, but she'd ignored it.

And that made her just as bad. By ignoring, she'd condoned. "Did Daddy know?"

"Oh, no. That was the point."

"Which I'm missing completely. Please, start at the beginning."

Lydia paced for a moment—another surprise. A lady through and through, her mother *never* paced.

"I didn't know what else to do, Jordan. You see

what the financial stress has done to your father's health. And I knew in my heart that you didn't really want to marry Randall."

Jordan's back teeth were beginning to ache. "How does having me kidnapped fix Daddy's finances and get me out of marrying Randall?"

"Don't you see?" Lydia's expertly made-up eyes welled with tears and she reached for Jordan's hands. "I did it for you, and for your father. Randall had money. The note was to be delivered to *him.* He would have paid for your return, Cyrus would have taken his cut and handed over the funds to me. I would have, in turn, given the money to your father, and he would not have had to grovel for a loan from those bank people."

Lydia released Jordan's hands and resumed pacing.

Jordan shook her head, still as confused as ever. "If Daddy wasn't in on it, where were you going to tell him you'd gotten your hands on this windfall? Wouldn't it be a little obvious after Randall had paid a demand and then you and Daddy had suddenly fallen into a fortune?"

"That's just it. Cousin Al would have delivered a document stating just such a thing—that I'd received an inheritance." Lydia sniffed. "It's well-known that my family has money."

"Then why didn't you just *ask* them for it?"

"Your father has his pride, dear."

"Pride?" she echoed, feeling as though she'd just executed a tricky jump and found out there was no solid ground on the other side of the fence.

"Really, Jordan. There's no need to raise your voice. I love you. I was thinking of you. You've always taken so many responsibilities on your shoulders, and I knew you'd agreed to marry Randall because of what he could do for your father. You gave your word, and it was tearing you up inside.''

But that didn't excuse this harebrained plot. And Jordan didn't want to consider the legalities of the matter. The feds had a tendency to frown on such things. Besides that, jailhouse orange was not Lydia's best color.

''I knew this was about money. But I didn't realize how ugly it was. I should never have let Tanner leave.'' Jordan was speaking more to herself now. ''I should have followed my heart.'' Then another thought struck her. Tanner must have known. Otherwise he would never have let her return.

She wasn't in danger from her own parents. Though misguided, Lydia had had her heart in the right place.

As Jordan watched—too astonished for the moment to object—Lydia struck a match. Hands shaking, she held it to the corner of the damning paper, then tossed the burning missive into the fireplace.

''I appreciate what that young man tried to do for you, but as I said, you were never in danger. You might think you have feelings for him—that happens quite frequently when a person is thrown into such a situation. Usually, it's a result of gratitude. Give it some time, and you'll come to realize that I'm right. Besides, your father would never go along with a liaison between you and the Caldwell boy.''

Stunned—when she had thought she was surely past the point—Jordan wasn't certain her voice would work. '''The Caldwell boy'?'' She rubbed at her temples, which were starting to ache. She told herself it no longer mattered what her parents thought, told herself she wouldn't ask.

She did anyway. "Why not?"

"Because of what his father did."

"His father..." Her words trailed off in sheer astonishment. "Are you talking about the fire?"

"Well, yes." She looked surprised that Jordan didn't "get it." "You know we've never recovered from that loss—and Douglas Caldwell was the likely suspect. So you understand why you mustn't mention Tanner Caldwell to your father anymore. The two of you have fought enough over this. He knows that you've spent the week with the boy, but he's willing to let it pass."

Anger winged out of nowhere, catching Jordan off guard. The emotion was so powerful, she couldn't speak for a moment.

And Tanner was far from a *boy*.

"You and Daddy are blaming Tanner for something you *believe* his father caused? And even so, if the man was drunk, that fire might not have been deliberately set. *And* Daddy was underinsured. He cut corners."

"Surely he did nothing of the sort." Now Lydia was as agitated as Jordan, wringing her hands and looking uncertain. "And show some respect, young lady. Your father has doted on you. He is a fair man."

"Fair?" A long-forgotten image surfaced. She'd been galloping across the meadow and had caught sight of Tanner talking to her father. Actually, her father had been doing the talking, or lecturing; Tanner had only stood there, silent, his shoulders stiffened with pride. Jordan had slowed her mount, thought to go over and speak with him. But Maynard had shouted an order at her—she couldn't even remember what it had been. And she hadn't considered disobeying.

She'd hesitated for an instant, and her gaze had locked with Tanner's. There had been embarrassment there, and anger, then his eyes had softened. For her. Turning his back on her father, he'd touched two fingers to his forehead in a soft salute.

It was the last she'd seen of him until that night in Gatlin's.

She realized now that her father had fired him, ordered him off Grazer land. That must have been the day Tanner had gone home to find his father gone, and the trailer missing.

Oh, Lord, because of who Tanner was, he'd been judged. And that was a terrible injustice.

Acceptance should never be measured by the status of one's family name.

She felt disgusted by the small-town bigotry, by how it could ruin a life. The sins of Tanner's father should not have reflected on the son.

And by damn, she was tired of living by the Grazer code, tired of keeping up appearances. She wanted out.

She wanted Tanner.

She stood, her decision made. "What did the doctor say about Daddy?"

The switch of subject had Lydia's brow clearing. "The EKG was normal, and there are no signs of a heart attack." Lydia smiled softly. "With a modified diet and a reduction of stress, he'll probably outlive us all."

Relief strengthened Jordan's determination. "Then, as gently as possible, I think you should tell him your part in this whole scheme."

Lydia's features crumpled as tears spilled over her lids, leaving shiny tracks in the matte of her face powder. "Oh, Jordan. I can't. What will he think of me? I did this for you—and for him. But I'm ashamed." She gripped the back of the damask-covered chair, her shoulders sagging as if weighted down by a burden too heavy to be borne. "I'm just so used to keeping up appearances."

Jordan touched her mother's arm, offering comfort, her anger vanishing at the sheer distress on her mother's beautiful face.

"We shouldn't *have* to keep up appearances, Mother. I've been guilty of the same thing, myself, and I intend to change that." Her voice softened. "Besides, Daddy loves you...and so do I."

"I'm so sorry for the mess I've caused. I only want your happiness, honey."

"I know, Mother." She wrapped her arms around Lydia, the familiar scent of Chanel bringing tears to her eyes. She was about to take a really big step, and frankly, it scared the daylights out of her. "And it's about time I took care of that happiness."

Lydia nodded, her eyes reflecting the true understanding of a mother. "Whatever you decide, I'll be here for you."

Jordan went out to the stables and used the phone there to make two calls. At last she was taking her life into her own hands—determined to live it for herself.

LUCKILY, RANDALL DIDN'T have any power lunches scheduled, and he made it out to the ranch within a half hour.

Jordan stepped outside the cool interior of the stables into the bright June sunshine and watched as he got out of his champagne-colored Mercedes. He really was a good man. Handsome. Gentle. Unassuming.

Why couldn't she love him?

"How's it going, beautiful?" Randall gave her a quick kiss on the cheek, grinned, then blew the smooth act by sneezing.

"Oh, Randall, I forgot about your allergies. I should have driven into town instead of having you come out here."

"No. This is fine. I took an antihistamine and it should kick in any time now."

He was so accommodating, Jordan thought she might cry. She swallowed and swiped at a fly that buzzed near her hair.

"You shouldn't have to live on allergy medication just to be around me."

"It's not that big a deal." He glanced at his watch.

"Isn't it? Randall, do you really want to marry me?"

"Of course—"

She touched the sleeve of his light gray suit. "*Really*, Randall? Please be honest."

He hedged, clearly caught off guard. His sky-blue eyes sharpened. "Are you saying you don't want to get married?"

Answering a question with a question was a sure indication of what she'd expected. His feelings were not engaged. Not in the way they should have been.

But Randall was ever diplomatic. He wouldn't needlessly cause pain.

"I hadn't said it yet, but yes," she admitted. "That about sums it up."

He looked a little surprised, a little unsure, but not hurt.

"You don't love me, Randall." She held up her hand when he started to speak. "And I care for you, but I can't love you the way you deserve. You're looking for a wife as an ornament who'll make you look settled in the eyes of your constituents. You don't need that, Randall…or me. You're a good man and your qualifications will speak for themselves."

He stared at her for a long moment. "I think that's what drew me to you. Your unswerving belief in the people you care about."

She tried for a smile. "That and the fact that the town *expected* us to be a couple?"

He chuckled. "A little like a comfortable old shoe, huh? Which, when examined in the bright sunlight, doesn't sound too complimentary." He glanced past her, looking at the stables that had always been her first and fiercest love. "Is it Caldwell?"

Just the mention of Tanner's name made her insides flutter. She nodded, surprised that he'd been astute enough, after all, to pick up on the undercurrents.

With a soft kiss on the back of her hand that stirred nothing stronger than the feeling of hugging a teddy bear, he said, "I hereby release you from your promise to marry me."

"Oh, that sounds awful. Broken promises. I've never—"

"I know," he interrupted. "Actually, I've got a job offer in the city. It'll bring me closer to where I want to be politically. I wasn't going to accept right away—at least, not until we'd settled a bit into the marriage, but now I think it's best. I'll do what I can about your father's loan."

Her eyes stung. "You don't need to. I've figured a way to cover him."

"You sure?"

She nodded.

"Okay. But if you ever need me... Well, keep in touch."

She kissed his cheek and watched as he got into his car and gave a jaunty wave. There was sadness—yes, a natural feeling when anything comes to an end. Sadness that though they'd tried, there just wasn't enough substance to keep a relationship like theirs afloat. Sadness about change.

And fear over that change, too.

Because ending her relationship with Randall was a speck of dust compared to the monumental step she was about to take.

She turned and made her way to Bleu's stall. Opening the latched door, she slipped her arms around the stallion's neck, pressed her face to his warm, sleek coat...and wept.

"I love you, Bleu."

Chapter Fourteen

Tanner had spent a week with the wind in his face and speed at his heels, trying to outrun the demons. The pain of being alone. Again.

And by God, it wasn't working. He couldn't do it, couldn't run far enough or fast enough. He couldn't give Jordan up without a fight.

The hypnotic streak of white lines on asphalt were a crooked blur now as he swung the Harley in a tight circle and poured on the speed in earnest. With purpose.

Pride was for idiots and he wasn't going to let it stand in his way any longer. He was in love with Jordan Grazer and it was time he told her so. If he had to kidnap her from the church steps a second time, he'd do it.

He had money and Jordan should know it. Grazer should know it. He'd *make* Maynard Grazer see that he was somebody, that he was right for Jordan. Even if he had to sit on the man to do it.

Background or not, no one would love her like he did. That should count for something in a parent's eyes.

In record time, he was pulling off the highway,

passing under the arched sign that proclaimed Grazer's stables and vineyards. He drove right up to the front door, beneath the fancy portico, booted the kickstand and hit the kill switch.

His knuckles stung with the force he used to rap on the double-door entry.

The door swung wide and the housekeeper's jaw dropped as he strode right past her. "Jordan!"

"She's not... She's—"

"Where is she?" Without waiting for a reply, he headed for the first hall that looked like it would lead to bedrooms.

"Wait!" Bess said, wringing her hands. "You mustn't—"

"Here, now, what's all the commotion?"

Tanner stopped, changed directions and came face-to-face with Maynard Grazer.

"Where's Jordan? And don't tell me you don't know."

Maynard hung his head. "That's exactly what I'm about to tell you."

Tanner was a breath away from losing his temper. Maynard's next words stopped him cold.

"You've saved me a lot of grief trying to track you down, and I'm glad as hell you're here now."

It was an effort not to let his astonishment show. But Tanner had learned never to trust an opponent. A person could stick you with a knife and smile while the blood ran.

"You were looking for me? Well, I'm here now. But I'm not in the mood for a civilized chat."

"I figured as much. And I don't blame you." Maynard gestured toward the den. "Why don't you step in here."

Tanner did, noticing that Maynard looked pale and agitated. He didn't know what possessed him to go to the sideboard and pour ice water into a crystal tumbler, but he did and handed it to his old nemesis.

"Thank you." Maynard drank, then set the glass aside.

"Where's Jordan?"

"She's gone. That's why I was attempting to contact you."

"She's not with me." Tanner's insides went from irritation to terror in record time. "When's the last time you saw her?" His voice softened dangerously. To those who knew him, it was a tone that could well describe a lethally coiled snake about to strike. "I want details, man."

"And I'll give you what I've got. The last time I saw her was right here in this den, early this morning—when she handed me a check from the sale of her stallion."

Stunned, Tanner wasn't even aware of dropping into a chair until he felt the support of leather beneath his thighs. "She what?"

"You heard me."

"Jordan wouldn't sell Honor Bleu. Not for anything."

"She would and she did. For you. Now I aim to get the damned beast back."

Tanner's mind was snagged a whole sentence behind. "What do you mean she sold the horse for me?"

"Not just the horse. She sold all her jewelry, and her car. Plunked down a check that damned near made my eyes pop out and told me I was a jackass—"

When Tanner frowned skeptically, Maynard backtracked.

"Well, she didn't exactly call me one, but the implication was there. She said the money was to pay for your debt and that if I had any decency in my heart, I'd consider the Caldwell part in our financial downfall square."

"My debt?" Tanner's grip tightened on the chair. He wasn't going to let the old shame take hold. He wasn't going to shoulder the blame or allow anyone to make him feel less of a man.

Obviously Maynard wasn't going to heap it. He held up a hand. "Hear me out before you comment. That's a damned feisty girl I raised and she's right more times than not. She said with this money, there wouldn't be any need for a bank loan—of which *she* was the collateral."

Tanner raised a brow, but refrained from commenting.

"My little girl told me in no uncertain terms that you might not have a whole lot of money, but that you've got more integrity than the whole bunch of us put together."

"Well, she might be a little off on the money reference."

Maynard didn't appear to hear, apparently still determined to relate every one of the sins Jordan had laid at his feet.

"I'm ashamed to admit that she was right about my lack of integrity. It took her selling that horse she loves so much to make me realize a few home truths. I cut corners and was underinsured when the fire wiped out the vineyards. I needed someone to blame, and you and your father were handy. I'm sorry for that. You deserved a better shake than I gave you.''

"My father was drunk on the job, Maynard. You were well within your rights to fire him. I'd have done the same.''

"Thank you for that. I don't expect you to excuse my behavior, but I'd like a chance to get to know you, Tanner. Any man who can affect my daughter so profoundly has to have high qualities. And for her sake, as well as my own, I'd like to try and form a friendship with you. But it'll have to wait for a bit. Right now, my priority is finding out where Samuel Bartholomew lives and buying back a certain stallion.''

"Mr. B. bought her horse?" The sly old fox hadn't said a word. Of course, Tanner had been busy licking his wounds, itching to run. He should have known Samuel would come to Jordan's rescue.

"Yes. And he paid top dollar, too. But I can't let her give up that horse. I've got to get it back.''

Tanner thought about his pride again. If he'd just told her about his money, none of this would have happened. Then again, maybe it would have. She wouldn't have accepted his money to bail her father out.

She'd needed to do that on her own.

But she'd had to shoulder too much, *be* too much for too many people. It was going to stop. They'd probably butt heads over what she would consider interference—and that was fine. He'd enjoy the skirmish.

"You were looking for a loan from a son-in-law," Tanner said. "I intend to be yours. I'll get the horse back.''

"Yes. That'll be faster. You know right where your friend lives." Maynard didn't even blink at Tanner's bold statement of intent. He merely held out the cashier's check that Jordan had given him.

It was a minute before Tanner could corral his surprise. "No. You keep that money. Consider it an investment. The investment you put into Jordan. It's obvious those years were grounded in love. She turned out to be one hell of a woman."

"But—"

"Reinvest the money into Grazer's holdings, Maynard. Build up your reserves. The horse will be my wedding gift to Jordan."

Maynard frowned. "I'll tell you right off that you have my blessing to marry my daughter. But can you afford such a purchase?"

Tanner hadn't asked for his blessing. That he'd gotten it—and before Maynard knew Tanner's true financial standing—went a long way to healing the rift that had begun so many years ago.

He grinned and rapped his knuckles on Maynard's desk. "I can afford it. Without it even making a ripple."

A LOW, THUNDEROUS rumble split the peacefulness of the little town. Jordan's heart leaped into her throat and her fingers curled around the cool satin of the wedding gown draped over her arm.

Shading her eyes, almost afraid to hope, she stood poised outside the pawnshop, reluctant to take that last step off the curb.

The din grew louder, vibrating in her chest, winging through her fluttering heart.

And that was when she saw him. Windswept hair

flowed behind him as he negotiated the powerful machine around the corner. Sunlight glanced off the gleaming chrome of the Harley-Davidson, outlining the impatience, the exquisitely determined features of his warrior's face.

He looked like a man bent on abduction. And Jordan figured she just might stand still for Tanner Caldwell's brand of stealing.

Because he'd stolen her heart some fifteen years back.

Mindful of her toes, she stayed where she was, bare inches from the curb, her gaze still riveted on the man she intended to persuade into marriage.

He crossed the yellow dividing lines of the asphalt—illegally—and came to an impressive, cocky halt, right in her pathway, shutting off the engine.

"How's it going, party girl?" Leaning his forearms on the handlebars, he gave her a wicked grin. "Heard you're a little short on wheels. Need a ride?"

Those killer dimples winked and her insides fluttered wildly. "I might."

"Where you headed?"

"Across the street." Coherency was next to impossible. Her mouth was as dry as dust and her palms were damp. She gave it a shot anyway. "There's a shop that specializes in dresses from around the country. I thought I'd see what kind of price I can get for this." With a nod of her head, she indicated the gown that was draped over her arm.

"Seems we've already been through a fair amount of grief over that dress and my bike. I don't suppose you'd stuff it in my duffel?"

Oh, she wanted to return that wicked smile. But he was way too sure of himself as it was. "Don't suppose."

He pulled his wallet out of his hip pocket. "How much?"

"For what?"

"The dress. I'll buy it. That way I can stuff the damned thing anywhere I want."

Her eyes narrowed. "You can't afford to be buying used wedding gowns."

"Don't bet on it, baby. How much?"

Okay. She'd play. "They gave me fifty to start with. It cost me seventy to get it back."

He gave a low whistle. "Should've never told the guy its true worth. I'll give you an even grand." He reached for her hand and slapped ten crisp one-hundred-dollar bills in her palm. Before she could protest or shut her slack jaw, he snatched the dress and crammed it into his duffel.

"Your mouth's hanging open, Blackie," he noted casually. "Did I forget to tell you I'm a flashy security expert? I'm even listed on the stock exchange." The dress didn't all fit in the khaki duffel. He didn't seem to care. "Get on."

Jordan shook her head, stunned. The stock exchange?

He sighed and fired the engine, then took the matter entirely out of her hands when he grabbed her arm and swung her on in front of him.

"What are you doing?" She scrambled for something to hold on to, then settled for the gas cap on the shiny black tank. An impromptu saddle horn, she thought, feeling a swift pang over giving up her horse.

He gunned the engine and brought the bike up to speed. "Grab the controls."

Surely she hadn't heard him correctly.

"I'm letting go," he warned, his breath warm against her ear.

"Do you have a death wish?" In a flash, her hands were on that bar. The jerky transition goosed the acceleration.

"No. More like a lifetime one." Now that his own hands were free, he wasted no time in caressing her thighs.

With her heart pounding like a winning Thoroughbred at Saratoga, and horribly afraid she'd send them into the ditch, she eased her grip on the throttle. The Harley slowed. She'd had it all planned. She would sell the dress, find Tanner, present him with the money and her heart, and beg him if need be to live happily ever after with her. Even if they had to do it in semi-poverty.

Her script had just been shredded beyond recognition. And she felt terribly off-balance.

"What's going on, Tanner?"

"You're kidnapping me."

"I am not."

"Looks that way to me. You're at the controls. A little more throttle, Blackie," he coached.

She twisted the rubber grip, secretly thrilled that he automatically assumed she could handle his powerful machine. He knew her well; knew that she rarely left anything to chance, that she preferred being the one who held the reins. By giving up the controls, he was letting her lead—to a point.

A smile stole through her insides and blossomed

on her face. This revised scenario might even be a better one.

"Kidnapping seems a solid plan," she said at last, feeling a giddy sense of joy. "Though I hope you know I'm broke."

"I'd heard that. How about we consider the grand for the dress a down payment on ransom?"

"I don't know, Tanner. That's a ten-thousand-dollar dress. You picked it up pretty cheap." Just for the sheer fun of it, she steered the Harley into a gentle snake pattern that zigzagged across the whole lane. "Where am I kidnapping you to, by the way?"

His arm around her waist tightened, but he didn't make a peep about her erratic driving. "Keep going. I'll guide you."

And he did, right to the acres of paddocks on Mr. B.'s estate, where her beloved stallion waited, a red bow wrapped around his neck, a white blanket tossed over his back.

Written in bold red ink were the words,

Marry Me, Blackie. I Love You.

She was barely aware of Tanner placing his hands over hers, bringing the motorcycle to a safe stop. If left up to her, they'd have fallen over like an animated tricycle in a comedy show.

Tears clogged her throat, trembled in her voice. "My horse wants to marry me?"

Tanner pressed his lips to her neck, then shifted her to face him on the bike. "What do you think?" he asked dryly.

"I'm overwhelmed. I can hardly breathe, let alone think. Did you give back Samuel's money?"

His hands were linked behind her back, her thighs straddling him. "In a manner of speaking. It was a little tough to figure the interest based on hours rather than days."

"He made you pay interest?"

"No. I offered a bonus. You're worth it. And I really *am* rolling in dough."

"You are?" She shut her eyes. That had sounded so mercenary.

He laughed, loud and deep—at her. With her. Those wonderful dimples cut sexy furrows in his whisker-dusted cheeks. He looked disreputable and just a little dangerous.

And he was all hers.

"My last financial statement showed thirteen million. But business is up this year. I'd estimate closer to fifteen."

"Fifteen…?" Her voice squeaked on a note of awe. "Million?"

"Give or take."

"I'm staggered."

"And I'm in love." He pressed his lips to hers, swept her hair behind her ear. "I'll buy you a stable of horses. The best around, not just the needy ones—although we can get those, too, if you want them. No matter what stock you choose, I've got faith in you. You'll make the best damned horse breeder around. Kentucky bluegrass country won't have anything over on you."

"We could go to Kentucky, if you want," she said, trying to get closer. That kiss wasn't nearly long enough. "Start over where nobody knows us."

He shook his head. "Sorry. There's a catch here. If you're going to breed horses, you'll need to do it in Grazer's Corners, or close to it, anyway. Seems the mayor's position could be up for grabs soon. I'm thinking I might just toss my hat in the ring.''

She couldn't have been more astonished if he'd told her he was an alien. "You want to be the mayor?"

"Sure. Why not? My offices practically run themselves. I've got great staff and more money than I know what to do with. I thought I'd take a stab at small-town life, and at mucking out stalls in my wife's stables.''

Jordan thought she might burst with happiness. Tanner had sworn he'd never settle back in Grazer's Corners. And she'd sworn she'd never leave. Their families had sworn they couldn't be together.

And that thought gave her pause, deflated her happy bubble just a little.

"My father—"

He placed a fingertip over her lips. "Your father and I have established a truce. We've even made a date to work on becoming bosom buddies.''

Jordan rolled her eyes. "Now I know you're getting carried away. When is this date?''

"After our wedding...provided you say yes, that is. You haven't yet.''

She gave a delighted laugh. "Yes. A hundred times, yes. If you hadn't asked, I'd have done it myself.''

"You were going to propose? Even thinking I was poor?''

"I don't want your money, Tanner. I want you.''

With melting tenderness, he cupped his hands around her face. "You've got me, baby. For life.

There's just one more small detail I need in order to seal this bargain.''

"What's that?'' She was sinking deeper into the velvety depths of his steady brown eyes.

"The words.''

"Words?''

"Yeah. Three of them.''

It took her a moment. The wondrous strength and heat he gave off was causing a short circuit in her brain. The rest of her nerve endings were humming along just fine "I haven't said it?''

"With your eyes, yes. But not with that sexy mouth.''

She stroked his long hair back from his face, traced the indent in his cheek where a dimple lurked. "I love you. Anywhere, anytime, always and in all ways, I love you.''

"That'll do.'' His voice was deep and low and shook with raw emotion. "That'll do just fine.'' He tossed his head, sending his long hair streaming, then cleared his throat. "If you trust Mr. B. with Honor Bleu for a few more days, I'll have him trailer the horse home for you.''

It wasn't often that she saw Tanner Caldwell shaken. That she'd caused it—with her words and with her love—gave her a fluttery feeling in the pit of her stomach that was almost too much to contain. "There's no need for Samuel to go through the trouble. I can come back with my own rig.''

His mouth canted at the corners—slowly and sexily. "I think he's looking for an excuse to get back to Grazer's Corners.''

"Agatha?''

"Agatha.''

Jordan laughed. "Oh, the town is going to be buzzing, for sure. Will you want a long engagement?" she asked slyly, knowing his answer. "Because if you don't, I happen to know for a fact that the church is available this Saturday."

"Forget it. I'm not taking any more chances with weddings in Grazer's Corners. We'll find the nearest justice of the peace and get the job done."

"Now that seems a shame," she said playfully. "You *did* just purchase a wedding dress, you know."

He gave her a look so hot she nearly melted. "I love you like hell, baby, but there's no way I'm wading through thirty-three buttons to get you naked."

She looped her arms around his neck. "I could make it worth your while."

He groaned and pressed her up against him. "We're gonna have a dozen kids at the rate we're going."

"Three at least," she allowed, climbing right onto his lap. It was a good thing he had his feet planted firmly on the ground, because she was definitely off-balance.

But that was one of the things she loved about Tanner. She could trust him to hold her, to never let her fall.

"You know, we might have a little problem talking Charity Arden into doing the photos. Though maybe her luck with botched weddings will change since we won't be using the church." Her mind was racing now. "And I can't help but feel a little guilty for being so happy with Kate Bingham still gone and all. Even though she's been in contact with Moose and says she's fine—"

"Jordan?"

"Hmm?"

"Can we talk about photographers and churches and missing school principals later?" He tugged her shirt from the waist of her jeans. "I'm trying to seduce you."

"Right here?"

"To start with."

His clever hands were lighting a fire too hot to ignore. The pasture was sheltered by a grove of trees, isolated from prying eyes. The only one to see was Honor Bleu, and he was parading around like a proud matchmaker, wearing a proposal blanket, and bobbing his head as though adding his equine blessing to the suggestion.

Jordan was thrilled to give in.

"Do carry on."

"I intend to."

And he did, proving very effectively that all her dreams—past, present and future—were forever wrapped up in this one incredible man.

THE BRIDES

MEN at WORK

All work and no play?
Not these men!

July 1998
MACKENZIE'S LADY by Dallas Schulze
Undercover agent Mackenzie Donahue's
lazy smile and deep blue eyes were his best
weapons. But after rescuing—and kissing!—
damsel in distress Holly Reynolds, how could
he betray her by spying on her brother?

August 1998
MISS LIZ'S PASSION by Sherryl Woods
Todd Lewis could put up a building with ease,
but quailed at the sight of a classroom! Still,
Liz Gentry, his son's teacher, was no battle-ax,
and soon Todd started planning some
extracurricular activities of his own....

September 1998
A CLASSIC ENCOUNTER
by Emilie Richards
Doctor Chris Matthews was intelligent, sexy
and *very* good with his hands—which made
him all the more dangerous to single mom
Lizette St. Hilaire. So how long could she
resist Chris's special brand of TLC?

Available at your favorite retail outlet!

MEN AT WORK™

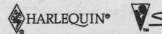 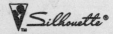

Look us up on-line at: http://www.romance.net   PMAW2

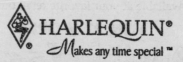

HARLEQUIN ULTIMATE GUIDES™

A series of how-to books for today's woman.

Act now to order some of these extremely helpful guides just for you!

Whatever the situation, Harlequin Ultimate Guides™ has all the answers!

#80507	HOW TO TALK TO A NAKED MAN	$4.99 U.S. ☐ $5.50 CAN. ☐	
#80508	I CAN FIX THAT	$5.99 U.S. ☐ $6.99 CAN. ☐	
#80510	WHAT YOUR TRAVEL AGENT KNOWS THAT YOU DON'T	$5.99 U.S. ☐ $6.99 CAN. ☐	
#80511	RISING TO THE OCCASION More Than Manners: Real Life Etiquette for Today's Woman	$5.99 U.S. ☐ $6.99 CAN. ☐	
#80513	WHAT GREAT CHEFS KNOW THAT YOU DON'T	$5.99 U.S. ☐ $6.99 CAN. ☐	
#80514	WHAT SAVVY INVESTORS KNOW THAT YOU DON'T	$5.99 U.S. ☐ $6.99 CAN. ☐	
#80509	GET WHAT YOU WANT OUT OF LIFE—AND KEEP IT!	$5.99 U.S. ☐ $6.99 CAN. ☐	

(quantities may be limited on some titles)

TOTAL AMOUNT	$
POSTAGE & HANDLING	$
($1.00 for one book, 50¢ for each additional)	
APPLICABLE TAXES*	$ _____
TOTAL PAYABLE	$ _____
(check or money order—please do not send cash)	

To order, complete this form and send it, along with a check or money order for the total above, payable to Harlequin Ultimate Guides, to: **In the U.S.:** 3010 Walden Avenue, P.O. Box 9047, Buffalo, NY 14269-9047; **In Canada:** P.O. Box 613, Fort Erie, Ontario, L2A 5X3.

Name: _____

Address: _____ City: _____

State/Prov.: _____ Zip/Postal Code: _____

*New York residents remit applicable sales taxes.
Canadian residents remit applicable GST and provincial taxes.

◆ HARLEQUIN®

Look us up on-line at: http://www.romance.net

HNFBL4

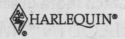

Not The Same Old Story!

Exciting, glamorous romance stories that take readers around the world.

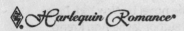
Sparkling, fresh and tender love stories that bring you pure romance.

Bold and adventurous—Temptation is strong women, bad boys, great sex!

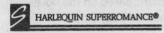
Provocative and realistic stories that celebrate life and love.

Contemporary fairy tales—where anything is possible and where dreams come true.

Heart-stopping, suspenseful adventures that combine the best of romance and mystery.

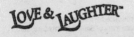
Humorous and romantic stories that capture the lighter side of love.